'Feel like some breakfast?'

That took the smile off her face. *'Don't!'* she implored, the mere thought of food making her stomach turn. 'Thank you anyway, Mr Cunningham,' she said sincerely—and saw his mouth twitch again. 'What...?' she began.

'We sleep together—and I'm still Mr Cunningham?' His grey eyes had the light of devilment in them.

'Not in that context!' she protested. 'We shared a room, that's—' She broke off—it had to be said that he'd seen more of her, in the literal sense, than any man she was on first-name terms with.

'I really think, Emily—' he took over when she seemed to be floundering '—that we know each other well enough for you to use my first name.'

Jessica Steele lives in a friendly Worcestershire village with her super husband, Peter. They are owned by a gorgeous Staffordshire bull terrier called Florence, who is boisterous and manic, but also adorable. It was Peter who first prompted Jessica to try writing, and, after the first rejection, encouraged her to keep on trying. Luckily, with the exception of Uruguay, she has so far managed to research inside all the countries in which she has set her books, travelling to places as far apart as Siberia and Egypt. Her thanks go to Peter for his help and encouragement.

Recent titles by the same author:

MARRIED IN A MOMENT
AGENDA: ATTRACTION!
A MOST ELIGIBLE BACHELOR
A WEDDING WORTH WAITING FOR

A NINE-TO-FIVE AFFAIR

BY
JESSICA STEELE

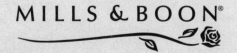

First published in Great Britain 1999
Harlequin Mills & Boon Limited,
Eton House, 18-24 Paradise Road, Richmond, Surrey TW9 1SR

© Jessica Steele 1999

ISBN 0 263 81689 3

Set in Times Roman 10½ on 11¼ pt.
02-9906-56525 C1

Printed and bound in Spain
by Litografia Rosés, S.A., Barcelona

CHAPTER ONE

SO MANY thoughts and emotions went through Emmie's mind as she drove to the job interview that winter's afternoon, chiefly how desperately she needed this position, and the tremendous hope that she would be successful in getting it. It didn't matter that it was only temporary—probably a maximum of nine months—it paid extremely well and would afford her some financial breathing space.

The work involved as assistant PA, and then acting PA while Mr Barden Cunningham's PA took maternity leave, would be very demanding, which accounted for the high salary. But, though Emmie had endured a blip in her career during this last year—well, several blips in actual fact—she knew, previous to that, her work record was exemplary.

Her secretarial training had been first class, and she had thought that, after three years with Usher Trading, she was really going places, and that she was due to be promoted as PA to one of the directors—only to go into work one Tuesday morning to learn, with utter astonishment, that the firm had folded. Usher Trading had, with a mile-long list of creditors, ceased trading.

It had not been her only shock that month. She had still been getting over her astonishment that, overnight, or so it seemed, Usher Trading had gone under, when her stepfather had suffered a heart attack and had died. The fact that she'd been without a job or financial security had been neither here nor there to her then. She had loved Alec Whitford as a daughter, and now he was gone.

Emmie clearly remembered her own father. He had been a scientist dedicated to his work, and for a lot of the time had seemed to be in a world of his own. He had also died, in some experiment that had gone wrong, when she had been ten years old.

Her life had been different then, Emmie recalled. Her family had lived in an elegant house in Berkshire and had been very comfortably off—sufficiently so for her mother to be able to indulge her love of antiques.

They'd had a whole houseful of beautiful furniture when, two years after her husband's death, her mother had married Alec Whitford. Alec had been a total contrast with Emmie's father. Alec had loved to laugh, and had been full of life, but—he hadn't liked work.

Though it hadn't been until after her mother's death three years later, in one of those freak garden machinery accidents that were never supposed to happen, that Emmie had begun to have any inkling that she and Alec were not financially sound.

She had been fifteen then. 'Shall I get a job, Alec?' she'd asked him, her thoughts on evening and weekend work.

'I wouldn't dream of it, sweetheart,' he'd said. 'We'll sell something.'

By the time she was eighteen, and had completed a most meticulous business training, there hadn't been much left to sell. By then Emmie had grown up fast to value security above all else. She'd loved her stepfather, and wouldn't have had him be any different, but he had seemed to make an art out of spending. She'd rather thought then—and later knew—that he was having a one-sided affair with his book-maker—Alec doing the giving, his bookmaker taking.

Emmie's mother had died intestate, so the house had passed to Alec. By that time Alec's mother, a formidable if slightly unconventional woman, had been living with them. Hannah Whitford had turned eighty, but was as sharp as a tack—and didn't suffer fools gladly. Emmie had calculated that she must be some kind of step-grandmother to her, but when out of respect she'd addressed her as Mrs Whitford, the thin, straight, white-haired woman had advised her that, since she drew the line at being called 'Granny', Emmie could call her Aunt Hannah.

So Aunt Hannah she had become. She had her own private pension—but, having already 'lent' her son her savings, had declined to let him see any of her pension. 'If you're that hard up,' she'd told him forthrightly when he'd come on the scrounge, 'sell the house!'

So he had. And they'd moved to a three-bedroomed rented apartment in a very nice area of London. And Emmie had started work at Usher Trading. All in all, given that Emmie had learned to more and more value her security, she had come to love Aunt Hannah too, and the next three years had passed very pleasantly.

And then Emmie had been made redundant and dear Alec had died. About that time, when Emmie had been trying to get a grip on things, she'd become startled to realise that Aunt Hannah was occasionally losing her grip a little!

At first Emmie had put it down to the fact that, for all Alec's mother had used to tear him off a strip from time to time, she had dearly loved him—and had lost him. Perhaps, when she had come to terms with her grief, she would be her old self again.

In the meantime, Emmie had found herself a new job with a firm of insurance brokers—and managed to hold it down for six weeks! Then her womanising boss, not content with the extra-marital affair he was having—the phone calls she'd overheard had spoken volumes—had had the utter nerve, after many ignored hints, to one day openly proposition *her*! That was when Emmie had discovered she was quite good in the tearing-off-a-strip department herself. Because, though it had been entirely unplanned, she'd been goaded beyond all possibility of suffering her new employer's lecherous advances any longer, she'd let fly with her tongue—and found herself out of a job.

She'd consoled herself that she didn't want to work there

anyway. And found herself another job. It had taken her ten weeks to lose it—this time for bad time-keeping. And it was true, her time-keeping *had* become appalling. But Aunt Hannah hadn't seemed to want to get out of bed in the morning any more and, while it had been no problem to take her breakfast in bed, Emmie had found she didn't love her work well enough to leave the apartment until she was sure Aunt Hannah was up and about.

Her third job after being made redundant from Usher Trading had lasted four months. It hadn't paid as well, but it had been nearer to her home, which had meant she hadn't had to leave for work so early. All had seemed to be well, until her employer's son had come home from abroad and, obviously believing himself to be irresistible, alternated between being overbearingly officious with her or, despite the fact he had a lovely wife and children, making suggestive, sickening remarks about how good he could be to her if she'd let him.

Emmie hadn't known how much more she could take, but supposed that working for fatherly Mr Denby at Usher Trading had rather sheltered her from the womanising types lurking out there. She'd recognised she was a novice at knowing how to handle them, and had been near to exploding again one day, when a call had come through from the local police station. Apparently they had a Mrs Hannah Whitford there, who seemed a little confused.

'I'm on my way!' Emmie exclaimed, holding down panic, grabbing up her bag, car keys at the ready.

'Where are you going?' Kenneth Junior demanded.

'Can't stop!'

'Your job?' he warned threateningly.

'It's yours—with my compliments,' she told him absently. The fact that she'd just walked out was the least of her worries just then. She made it to the police station in record time. 'Mrs Whitford?' she enquired of the man at the front desk.

'She's having a cup of tea with one of the WPCs,' he replied, and explained how the elderly lady had been found wandering the streets in her bedroom slippers and seemed distressed because she couldn't remember where she lived.

'Oh, the poor love!' Emmie cried.

'She's all right now,' the police officer soothed. 'Fortunately she had her handbag with her, and we were able to find your office telephone number in her spectacle case.'

'Oh, thank goodness I thought to jot it down!' Emmie's exclamation was heartfelt. She'd only put it in Aunt Hannah's spectacle case because she'd known the dear soul would look first for her glasses before she thought to look for her phone number.

'Has Mrs Whitford been—er—forgetful for very long?' the policeman asked in a kindly fashion. Emmie explained how, if Aunt Hannah had, it was only recently, and only since she had lost her son earlier in the year. Whereupon, on learning that Emmie was away from the apartment for most of the day, the officer tentatively suggested that it might be an idea to consider establishing Mrs Whitford in a residential home.

'Oh, I couldn't possibly!' was Emmie's initial shocked reaction. 'She would hate it!' And, getting over her shock a little, she asked, 'Was she very upset when you found her?'

'Upset—confused, distressed—and,' he added with a small smile, 'just a little aggressive.'

'Oh, dear,' Emmie mumbled feebly. But, fully aware that Aunt Hannah had a tart tongue when the mood took her, was in no mind to have Alec's mother 'established' in a residential home. Even if, while waiting for Aunt Hannah, the kindly policeman did suggest to her not to dismiss the notion out of hand, that residential homes weren't jails, and that if those in charge knew where residents were, they were quite at liberty to come and go as they pleased. For unintentional but added weight, he mentioned that while indoors someone was there all the time to keep an eye on residents, and see to it that they had their lunch.

Hannah Whitford suddenly appeared from nowhere. 'All this fuss!' she snapped shortly, quite back to normal, but Emmie, who knew her well, knew that she was more embarrassed than cross. 'Have you got your car outside?'

Emmie was not about to give the police officer's 'residential home' suggestion another thought. But Aunt Hannah, either having had a similar conversation with the woman police constable who'd looked after her, or having done some serious thinking of her own, brought the subject up herself. It was around lunchtime the following day that, having been deep in thought, Aunt Hannah suddenly seemed to realise that Emmie was not at work.

'What are you doing home?' she demanded in her forthright way.

'I thought I'd look for another job,' Emmie replied, aware that, with yesterday's confusion behind her, Aunt Hannah was getting back to being as sharp as she had ever been.

'Because of me.'

It was a statement, and despite Emmie telling her that she would have walked out of her job anyway, without receiving the phone call from the police station, Aunt Hannah would not have it.

Nor would she countenance—despite Emmie's protestation—that she should become a burden to her stepgranddaughter. But it was only when Emmie saw that she was growing extremely agitated that she agreed—more in the hope of calming her down than anything—to investigate the possibility of her step-grandmother moving to a residential home.

Aunt Hannah, as Emmie later realised—and might have known—was not prepared to stop at mere investigation. So they set off doing the rounds of residential homes. The first one they looked at, Keswick House, was in actual fact a very pleasant surprise. Light and airy, with its residents seemingly busy with their own pursuits, and a general cheerful atmosphere about the place. All residents were encouraged to bring their own furniture. There was, however, one very big drawback—it was expensive. To stay there was going to take all of Mrs Whitford's income and more.

With Aunt Hannah not ready to give up the idea, they began to look at other establishments. By then Emmie was starting to realise that, if she herself was out all day—as she would be when she found herself a new job—perhaps as a legacy of when Aunt Hannah had forgotten where she lived that day, the old lady would be frightened and nervous of being on her own. Aunt Hannah, Emmie all at once knew, needed to feel safe.

But, in adjusting to the fact that the dear soul was determined to move out, Emmie was not prepared to let her go and live just anywhere. The trouble was, though, that while one or two of the places they looked at were adequate, there were others that Emmie would not dream of allowing her step-grandmother to move to.

Emmie couldn't bear the thought that Aunt Hannah might feel frightened and unsafe in their apartment. She blamed herself that, when clearly Aunt Hannah needed company, she had left her on her own for so many hours during the day. But—Emmie had to work.

It wasn't until the following day, when Aunt Hannah had another spell of confusion—and came out of it looking very bewildered—that Emmie knew for sure what had to be done. How, for goodness' sake, would Aunt Hannah have coped if she'd been out at work? Aunt Hannah had to feel safe! Emmie rang Lisa Browne, the owner of Keswick House.

A week later, on the day before Emmie started her new job, Mrs Whitford moved into Keswick House. Fortunately, what with packing her personal treasures and looking forward to the move, she had entirely forgotten the stated fee required, and was happy to sign anything Emmie gave her and to leave all the paperwork to her step-granddaughter. Two weeks after that Emmie moved out of the well-maintained three-bedroomed apartment that had been the family home, to a two-bedroomed flat in a much less salubrious area.

Emmie ignored the peeling paint and the rotting woodwork of the front door, and strove to think positively. The house was old; what did she expect? Anyhow, because of its age, it would set off her few remaining pieces of antique furniture a treat. Well, it would when she'd stripped the walls and redecorated. And also, don't forget, it was a ground-floor flat—ideal for when Aunt Hannah, who wasn't so good with stairs, came to stay. As an extra bonus, it was only half the rent of the former apartment, so, providing she hung on to her new job at Smythe and Wood International, she could just about scrape up the shortfall required to keep Aunt Hannah at Keswick House.

A month later, however, and Emmie was having a hard time in staying optimistic. Her new flat was looking super. Newly decorated, with carpets and curtains as well as her mother's good quality furniture, which had transformed it. Emmie had become friends with Adrian Payne, the man who had the upstairs flat. Non-licentious Adrian, who was true to his ex-live-in-girlfriend Tina, had in part restored her faith in men.

Not completely, however. For her new boss, Clive Norris, turned out to be the womanising type she had just about had enough of. Her job at Smythe and Wood, it had to be said, was just not working out. While the tasks were no problem—she had a quick brain and absorbed instruction easily—she couldn't help wondering what was wrong with some of these men that they had to touch her, to hint—more than hint in some cases—that they'd quite care to be more than boss-PA-friendly.

Or, was it her? She didn't think so. She was sure she

didn't go around giving off come hither signals. She knew she hadn't been at the back of the queue when looks had been handed out. Alec had once declared she was utterly beautiful, but he had been in one of his happy moods. Though she *had* taken herself off to the mirror to check. Slender, five feet eight in bare feet, she had studied her flawless complexion, her straight, shoulder-length black hair, and looked into her liquid brown eyes. And then grinned, revealing perfect white teeth, and concluded that her stepfather had been just a little bit biased in her favour.

All this came back to her now, as she pulled into the car park of Progress Engineering for her interview. She was early. Emmie sat in her car, reflecting how disastrous everything had been just lately.

Needing the money she had doggedly stuck it out at Smythe and Wood, but she hadn't liked working for Clive Norris. Nor, to start with, had Aunt Hannah settled at Keswick House very easily. She disliked rules, and either by accident or design forgot to note in the 'Out' book where she was going when she went for a morning's short walk.

She invariably returned before anyone started to get anxious, but Emmie had received several phone calls to say Mrs Whitford had disappeared without saying where she was going, and had been absent some hours now, and they were starting to be concerned that she hadn't returned. Emmie had given Aunt Hannah a key to the new flat, and on that first occasion Emmie had to leave her office and hare back to the flat—Aunt Hannah hadn't been there. Thinking that perhaps Aunt Hannah might have returned to their old apartment, Emmie had rushed there, and with overwhelming relief had found her there, chatting, as nice as you please, to one of their former neighbours.

Emmie had Aunt Hannah to stay with her at the weekends, yet, despite her becoming familiar with the new area, whenever her step-grandmother did her disappearing act from Keswick House it was never to Emmie's new flat in the run-down area that she made for, but always their previous apartment.

But now, two and a half months after moving into Keswick House, Aunt Hannah seemed to have settled down. In fact, Emmie hadn't had to have any unexpected time off in the last two weeks. Until yesterday. She'd had Aunt Hannah with her for an extended weekend, and the plan had been to return her to Keswick House, five miles away, on Monday morning. But Emmie had overlooked the fact that her step-grandmother was never in any hurry to start her day, the result being that Emmie had been an hour late in getting to work yesterday.

She always worked late to make up for any time she had off. But yesterday, unfortunately, so too had Clive Norris. 'We could be doing better things than this,' he hinted, coming over and causing her to have to move away from the filing cabinet by which she was standing. 'Come and have a drink with me,' he went on, managing to make it sound more suggestive than a suggestion as he backed her into a corner.

'No, thanks,' Emmie replied, coolly but politely—and she saw Clive's expression change.

He didn't like it. 'You're too stuck-up by half,' he said nastily. 'You want taking down a peg!' he went on resentfully. And while she stood there feeling uncomfortable, wishing he'd go home and leave her in peace, to her absolute amazement the next thing she knew was that he made a grab for her and tried to kiss her.

His wet, lascivious lips made her heave. She wasn't thinking by then, but reacting—and her reaction was swift and immediate. She hit him with full force, and compounded that by giving him a furious push away from her. He ended up on the floor—looking ridiculous. He didn't like that either.

She stepped over him, grabbing up her coat and her bag. 'Goodnight!' she exploded, already on her way.

'Don't come back!' he screamed after her. He should be so lucky!

An hour later she calmed down, knowing that while she couldn't regret what she had done at the same time she simply couldn't afford to have done it. Not that she was going to ask for her job back. The thought of working for Clive Norris again made her shudder.

There had been just one letter in the post on Tuesday morning. She'd opened it and very nearly weakened in her resolve not to ask for her job back. Her letter was from Keswick House. One of the larger rooms had become available and Mrs Whitford had asked to transfer—would that be in order? Emmie had read on down, taking in the increased charge of the room. Oh, heavens, she couldn't afford it; she really couldn't. Well, not unless she managed to find a much better-paid job than the one she'd just walked out of. Clearly Aunt Hannah just hadn't taken into consideration when deciding that she'd like to move to a larger room that it would be more expensive.

Emmie went out and bought a paper and scanned the Situations Vacant column. One job had stood out from all the rest—assistant and then acting PA. The salary alone suggested it would be to someone very high up. She could do it, she knew that she could, and the salary named was beyond her wildest imaginings. The only snag was that the post was to cover maternity leave, and as such was only temporary. Emmie put the paper aside—then picked it up again as it dawned on her that so far over these last twelve months the longest she'd stayed anywhere had been four months. To work somewhere while covering maternity absence was starting to sound more like permanence to her. Besides which, if she had this sort of a salary coming in Aunt Hannah could move into the larger room and would perhaps be even more settled.

And, anyhow, Progress Engineering was no twopenny-halfpenny firm. The company were well-known in the mechanical and electronic engineering field. Surely, if she proved herself as good as Mr Denby had always said she was, might they find a niche for her within the organisation when the PA returned from maternity leave?

First, though, get the job. Hoping against hope that anyone better qualified would be more career-minded than to want to apply for a temporary job, Emmie picked up the phone and dialled. 'You're available straight away?' the head of Human Resources to whom she spoke had enquired efficiently.

'That's correct,' she'd answered, having not yet worked out what reason she was going to give for leaving her previous employer.

'Can you come and see me this afternoon?'

My word—they didn't hang about at Progress Engineering! 'Yes, of course,' she'd replied.

And now she discovered, as she sat before Mr Garratt, that the post she was applying for was not only as assistant and acting PA, but to Mr Barden Cunningham, the head of the whole conglomerate no less! The reason they weren't hanging about getting someone in was because Dawn Obrey, who was in around the fifth month of her pregnancy, was starting to have a few complications which, together with her antenatal appointments, meant she was out of the office quite a lot—sometimes very unexpectedly.

'Which, as you can appreciate—' Mr Garratt smiled '—is not always so convenient in the running of an extremely busy office. We've been able to switch people from other departments, of course, but Mr Cunningham prefers his own team.'

'That's quite understandable, from a continuity standpoint,' Emmie put in, having stretched the truth a mile by saying she had taken temporary jobs this past year to gain experience in many branches of industry. She had felt that her interview was going well, but owned to feeling a little let down when, the interview over, Mr Garratt stood up and, shaking her hand, advised her that he had two other candidates to see, but would be in touch very quickly.

Emmie drove home from her interview feeling very despondent. She hadn't known that the job was as PA to the head of the whole outfit. Barden Cunningham would want someone older; she was sure of it. Which was unfair, because she was good at her job; she knew she was.

By the time she reached her flat Emmie was convinced that she hadn't a hope of being taken on by Barden Cunningham. And though she knew that she should straight away ring Keswick House, and give some kind of reason why Aunt Hannah should not move into a larger room, somehow she could not.

Mr Garratt had said he would be in touch very quickly, but Emmie saw little point in holding her breath or looking forward to opening tomorrow's post. She knew how it would read: 'Thank you very much for attending for interview, but…'

A few hours later Emmie was again scanning the Situations column when the phone rang. Aunt Hannah had a phone in her room, but it wouldn't be her because as far as she knew Emmie was out at work. Emmie picked up the phone, 'Hello?' she answered pleasantly, trying not to panic that it might be Lisa Browne or one of the care assistants ringing to say Mrs Whitford had gone missing.

There was a small silence, then, 'Emily Lawson?' queried a rather nice all-male voice.

'Speaking,' she answered carefully.

'Barden Cunningham,' he introduced himself—and Emmie only just managed to hold back a gasp of shock.

'Oh, hello,' she said, and cringed—she'd already said hello once!

He came straight to the point. 'I should like to see you Friday afternoon. Are you free?'

'Yes, of course,' she answered promptly, her heartbeat

starting to pick up with excitement. 'What time would suit you?'

'Four-thirty,' he replied. 'Until then,' he added, and rang off—and Emmie's face broke out into one huge grin. She had an interview with no less a person than the top man himself!

She was still grinning ten minutes later. Mr Garratt had said he would be in touch very quickly—indirectly, he had been. He must have reported back to his employer the moment he had concluded all interviews. And, not waiting for mail to reach her, Barden Cunningham had phoned her within a very short space of time.

Which told her two things. One, that despite there being other candidates she was still in there with a chance. The other, that Progress Engineering were anxious to fill the temporary vacancy with all speed. Though from what Mr Garratt had said she thought she knew that already. Oh, roll on Friday; the suspense was unbearable.

Adrian Payne asked her to go out with him for a bite to eat on Thursday evening, but Emmie put him off. She wanted to be bright-eyed and bushy-tailed the next day for her interview, and intended to have an early night.

She was in frequent telephone contact with Aunt Hannah, but had not discussed her aunt's desire to move into a larger room, nor had she yet answered the letter from Lisa Browne at Keswick House. She knew, however, that she would have to ring Lisa Browne soon; courtesy if nothing else meant she should give some indication of whether or not Aunt Hannah could move. But pride, Emmie supposed, decreed that no one should know how desperately hard up she was but herself.

She was again early for her interview on Friday, and sat in her car for some minutes composing herself. She had on her best all wool charcoal-grey business suit, her crisp white shirt ironed immaculately.

She stepped from her car, knowing that she looked the

part of a cool, efficient PA in her neat two-and-a-half-inch heels, but felt glad that no one could know of the nervous commotion going on inside her. So much depended on this interview—and its outcome.

'My name's Emily Lawson. I've an appointment with Mr Cunningham at four-thirty,' she told the smart woman on the reception desk.

Emmie rode up in the lift, trying to stifle her nerves, desperate to make a good impression and hoping against hope that Mr Cunningham would turn out to be fatherly, like old Mr Denby. He hadn't sounded particularly fatherly over the phone, though.

Oh, she did so hope he was not another womaniser! She couldn't be that unlucky yet again, could she? Emmie pulled her mind away from such thoughts. She must concentrate only on this interview and Aunt Hannah, and the fact that if she was successful this afternoon Aunt Hannah could move into the double room she preferred.

Emmie made a vow there and then that, for Aunt Hannah's sake, if her prospective employer was yet another of the Casanova types she would keep a tight rein on her new-found temper. To do so would also mean that she kept her security—always supposing she was lucky enough to get the job. Having spent many years in a financially uncertain household, security was now more important to her than ever. She *had* to be self-reliant; she had no family but Aunt Hannah. And, having Aunt Hannah to look out for, Emmie knew she must think only of her career and, if all went well, the high salary being offered, which would afford both her and Aunt Hannah that security.

She was worrying needlessly, Emmie considered bracingly as she stepped out of the lift. This was a very different sort of company from the one she had walked out of on Monday—true, she had been told not to come back. But the very air about this place was vastly more professional.

Emmie found the door she was looking for, tapped on it

lightly and went in. A pale but pretty pregnant woman somewhere in her early thirties looked up. 'Emily Lawson?' she enquired.

'Am I too early?' Emmie's hopes suffered a bit of a dent. He'd want someone older; she felt sure of it.

'Not at all,' Dawn Obrey responded with a smile. And, leaving her chair, she went on, 'Reception rang to say you were on your way up. Mr Cunningham will see you now.'

Emmie flicked a hasty glance to the clock on the office wall, saw with relief that there were a few minutes to go before four-thirty and that neither her car clock nor her watch had played her false, and followed the PA over to a door which connected into another office.

'Miss Lawson,' the PA announced, and as Emmie went forward into the other room Dawn Obrey retreated and closed the door.

'Come in. Take a seat,' Barden Cunningham invited pleasantly, leaving his seat and shaking hands with her.

Ten out of ten for manners, Emmie noted with one part of her brain, while with another part she saw that Barden Cunningham was not old or fatherly, but was somewhere in his middle thirties. He was tall, had fairish hair and grey no-nonsense sort of eyes, but—and here was the minus— he was seriously good-looking. In her recent experience good-looking men were apt to think they were God's gift to women—and Barden Cunningham was more good-looking than most.

Emmie took a seat on one side of the desk and he resumed his seat on the other. His desk was clear, which indicated to her that he wouldn't be hanging about to start his weekend once this interview was over. Was she the last candidate?

She looked across at him and found he was studying her. She met his look, her large brown eyes steady, wishing she could read his mind, know what he was thinking. 'You're young,' he said. Was he accusing? He had obviously scanned the application form she had been asked to complete so knew she was twenty-two.

'I'm good,' she replied—this was no time to be modest!

He looked at her shrewdly, 'You trained at...' he began, and the interview was under way. His questions about her work experience, her views on confidentiality, were all clear, and most professional. 'What about your diplomacy skills?' he wanted to know.

Emmie knew that great tact was sometimes needed when dealing with awkward phone calls or difficult people. Now didn't seem the time to mention that earlier in the week diplomacy had gone by the board when she'd belted her previous boss and left him sprawled on the floor.

'Very good,' she answered, looking him in the eye. Well, they were—normally. Anybody who made a grab for her the way Clive Norris had, deserved what they got in her book. Barden Cunningham asked one or two more pertinent questions with regard to her general business knowledge, which she felt she answered more than adequately. 'When I worked at Usher Trading, communication skills were...' She went to expand when he stayed silent, only to be interrupted.

'Ah, yes, Usher Trading—they went into liquidation about a year ago,' he cut in—just as though it was her fault! As if she had been personally responsible!

Emmie clamped down hard on a small spurt of anger. Steady, steady, she needed this job. Perhaps he was just testing her to see how she reacted to the odd uncalled-for comment.

'Unfortunately, that's true,' she replied, and gave him the benefit of her full smile—which had once been called ravishing.

He was unimpressed. He looked at her, his eyes flicking from her eyes to her mouth and back to her eyes. He paused for a moment before, questions on her abilities seemingly over, he went on to refer to her work record over the past year. She'd had small hope that he would not do so. But, until she knew if this man was in the same womanising mould, Emmie didn't think she would be doing herself any favours if she gave the true reasons for her previous 'temporary' employment.

'As I mentioned to Mr Garratt—' she started down the path of untruth without falter '—I felt, having worked for the same firm for three years, that I should widen my work experience.' Usher Trading were no longer in existence, but if he wrote elsewhere for references—she was dead!

'Which is why you applied for this temporary post?'

There weren't any flies on him! 'I'm very keen to make a career in PA work,' she answered.

'You live with your parents?' he enquired out of the blue. She wasn't ready for it, and for a brief second felt unexpectedly choked.

She looked quickly down at her lap, swallowed, and then answered, 'My parents are dead.'

His expression softened marginally. 'That's tough,' he said gently. But after a moment he was back to being the interrogator. 'As I'm sure Mr Garratt mentioned, Mrs Obrey, my PA, is having an atrocious time of it at the moment. While in normal circumstances she would frequently accompany me when I need to visit our various other concerns, she isn't up to being driven around the country. That role will now fall to her assistant.' He fixed her with his straight no-nonsense look. 'Would that be a problem?'

Emmie shook her head. 'Not at all,' she answered unhesitatingly, hoping with all she had that Aunt Hannah's forgetful perambulations were a thing of the past. She'd been so good lately.

'It could be that I'd be late getting back to London,' Barden Cunningham stressed—and, those direct eyes on her still, he went on, 'You have no commitments?'

Emmie hesitated, but not for long. She guessed he meant

was she living with anyone. Now, if she was going to confide in him about Aunt Hannah, was the time to do so. 'None at all,' she replied, again managing to look him in the eye. Well, her security was on the line here—her chances of getting this job would go cascading down the drain if he had so much as an inkling of her previous bad time-keeping and the erratic work hours she'd kept.

'You'd have no problem working extra hours?'

Her heart lifted—the fact that this was turning out to be no cursory interview gave her confidence that she was still in there with a chance. 'Working extra hours, working late has never been a problem,' she replied, back on the honesty track, and glad that she was.

'You were called on to work late in your other temporary job?' he questioned, before she'd barely finished speaking—was he sharp or was he sharp!

'I never liked to go home before I'd got everything cleared,' she answered—oh, grief, that sounded smug and self-satisfied! Better, though, than telling him she'd regarded her jobs more as permanent than temporary during her short stays there.

Barden Cunningham had very few other questions he wanted to ask, and then he caused her hopes to go sky-high. 'When would you be available to start?' he wanted to know.

'Straight away,' she answered promptly.

'You've nothing else lined up for Monday?'

Oh, crumbs—had she answered too promptly? Emmie took a deep and steadying breath and then, her innate honesty rushed to the fore. 'Well, to be quite frank, I was hoping this interview would go well enough for me not to need to apply for anything else.'

Again Emmie wished she could have a clue as to what he was thinking. But he was giving nothing away as he sat and stared at her. Then, after some long moments, 'You want the job?' he enquired.

He'd never know how much. She swallowed down the word 'desperately' and changed it to, 'Very much.'

Barden Cunningham's eyes searched her face for perhaps another couple of seconds. Then slowly he smiled, and it was the most wonderful smile she had ever seen. But better than that were the words that followed, for, as he stood up, indicating the interview was over, he said, 'Then, since you're going to be working with her for a while, you'd better come and have a chat to Dawn.'

'I've got the job?' she asked, hardly daring to believe it.

'Congratulations,' he said, and shook her hand.

CHAPTER TWO

FEBRUARY was on its way out and they were in the throes
of some quite dreadful weather. Last week it had seemed
to rain non-stop. Today it had gone colder, and snow was
threatened. Emmie had not slept well, and got out of bed
that Wednesday morning feeling oddly despondent. Oh,
buck your ideas up, do. A month ago she had been over-
joyed that she'd actually managed to be offered the job of
assistant, shortly to be acting, PA to Mr Barden
Cunningham. So—what had changed?

Emmie padded around her flat, trying to pin-point why
she felt so—well, not exactly dissatisfied with her lot, but
certainly sort of restless, out of sorts about something.

Which was odd, because she no longer had any worries
about her step-grandmother. Aunt Hannah was now cheerfully established in the double room she had so wanted,
and was more settled than Emmie could have hoped.
Indeed, so content did Aunt Hannah seem that Emmie realised how right she had been to think it was important to
the dear soul to feel safe during the long hours while
Emmie was away at work. Safely ensconced in Keswick
House, gradually, bit by bit, Aunt Hannah's confidence was
returning. Her confidence—and her spirit of independence.
Twice in the last month Aunt Hannah had declined to stay
with Emmie for the weekend—though she had permitted
Emmie to collect her for Sunday tea.

So it wasn't on Aunt Hannah's account that she felt so
unsettled, Emmie decided. Her thoughts turned to her job,
and how, without bothering to take up references—clearly
he was a man confident in his own judgement, and that had

been one tremendous worrying hurdle out of the way—
Barden Cunningham had appointed her.

She had been working at the head office of Progress
Engineering for four weeks and two days now, and loved
the work. Had, in fact, taken to it like a duck to water.
Sometimes she worked under pressure but she absorbed it,
enjoyed the challenge—and felt that she did well enough
that her employer could not have one single solitary com-
plaint about her output.

She got on exceedingly well with Dawn and was glad to
be of help to her whenever she could, because, as well as
being a thoroughly nice person, Dawn was not having a
very easy pregnancy at all. 'I thought morning sickness was
something that happened early on—not now,' Dawn had
sighed only yesterday, after yet another visit to the ladies'
room.

'Why not go home? There's nothing here I can't cope
with,' Emmie had urged.

'I'll stick it out,' Dawn had said bravely. 'I'm having
tomorrow afternoon off for an antenatal appointment, as
you know. Thanks all the same, Emmie.'

Dawn had asked her that first Monday if she was called
Emily or if there was another name she was known by.
'I've been called Emmie for as long as I can remember,'
she'd answered, and had been Emmie to all at Progress
Engineering since then.

So, Emmie went back to trying to find the root cause of
what was making her so restless. She had no worries about
Aunt Hannah now, she liked her job and she liked Dawn,
and everything else was ticking along nicely. So why did
she feel…?

Her thoughts suddenly faltered. Everybody at Progress
Engineering called her Emmie—except *him*! To him, she
was still Emily. She wasn't terribly sure quite when Barden
Cunningham had become *him*. She had quite liked him during those first few hours of working for him. That was

before she had taken the first of his May-I-speak-with-Barden-please-Paula-here-type calls.

'Do I put Paula through?' she'd whispered to Dawn.

There had followed, over the next few weeks, Ingrid, Sarah, and a whole host of other females—it was a wonder to Emmie that he ever got any work done. But he did. That was the bitter pill. She couldn't fault him; given that—wouldn't you know, another wretched womaniser—he took time out to answer his calls, the amount of work he turned out was staggering.

'He's not married, then?' Emmie had asked Dawn, knowing she was going to hate him like the devil if he were.

Dawn had shaken her head. 'Why limit yourself to one pudding when you can have the whole dessert trolley?'

Emmie had managed a smile, but she'd had her fill of womanisers. She'd been sure, however, to keep her feelings well hidden, but happened to be in his office when a female she hadn't so far come across had telephoned him.

'Claudia!' he'd exclaimed with pleasure. And, charming the socks off Claudia—Emmie didn't want to know what else he charmed off her—he'd kept Emmie waiting while he dallied with his new love.

'If you'd just sign these papers for me!' Emmie had requested crisply, when he'd at last finished his call.

She'd ignored his raised eyebrow, that look that said, Who the blazes do you think you are? 'Anything else?' he'd asked sarcastically, and Emmie had felt sorely inclined to give him a taste of what she'd given Clive Norris.

'No, thank you,' she'd replied politely, if a shade aloofly, and returned to her desk. Men!

True, he hadn't attempted the womanising bit with her. Let him try! Not that she wanted him to. Heaven forbid! It irked, though, in some strange way that he still called her Emily, even though she knew for a fact that to him, Dawn always referred to her as Emmie.

Realising she was getting all huffy and puffy over nothing, Emmie got ready to face the day and drove herself to work. The morning went well, and Dawn went off at lunchtime to keep her hospital appointment.

Barden Cunningham was out of the office for the first hour of that afternoon, and Emmie quite enjoyed the challenge of being left in sole charge of the office. Her enjoyment, however, was somewhat dimmed by a telephone call she took around two-thirty.

'Mr Cunningham's office,' she said into the mouthpiece, on picking up the phone.

'Roberta Short,' the caller announced herself. 'That's Emmie, isn't it?' See—even Cunningham's friends knew she was called Emmie!

'Yes,' she answered, a smile in her voice. She liked Roberta Short, a striking woman in her early thirties. Emmie had met her and her husband, a man in his late forties, when they had called in to see her employer one day. 'I'm afraid Mr Cunningham isn't in.'

'Oh, drat! I particularly wanted to catch him.'

'May I get him to call you?' Emmie offered—and felt her blood go cold at Roberta Short's panicky reply.

'Lord, no!' she squeaked. 'Neville mustn't know I'm phoning Barden. I've an idea he already suspects—' She broke off. 'Oh, help, Neville's coming in... He mustn't find out...' The line went dead.

Slowly, feeling stunned, Emmie replaced her phone. No, she'd got it wrong. That call just now didn't really imply what she'd thought it might. Neville Short was Barden Cunningham's friend, for heaven's sake! Just because Cunningham was a womaniser of the first order, it didn't follow that even married women weren't safe from him. Emmie felt all churned up inside. Why didn't it? He had charm by the truckload—no woman was safe from him. Well, save for her, and she was sure that didn't bother her in the smallest degree!

But—his friend's wife? No! Emmie got on with some work, but time and again those words 'I've an idea he already suspects' and 'Neville's coming in… He mustn't find out…' before Roberta Short had abruptly ended her call returned to haunt her.

Ignore it. It's nothing to do with you even if he is having an affair with his friend's wife. Two-timing her too with Claudia whatever-her-name-was, who'd phoned him last week. The man was an out and out monster! Men like him wanted locking up!

The sound of the connecting door to the next office opening told her that the object of her sweet thoughts was back. Who had he been extending his lunch with? she'd like to know. Claudia? Paula?

Emmie looked up. 'Any messages?' Barden Cunningham wanted to know.

'Mrs Neville Short rang,' Emmie replied. 'She didn't want to leave a message.'

'She'll ring again, I expect.'

My stars! How about that for confidence? Though, since the diabolical hound most likely knew that Neville Short was at home, he wouldn't be likely to ring Roberta while her husband was there. Emmie concentrated solely on being an efficient PA, and then told her employer of a business enquiry she'd taken before he went back to his own office and closed the door. She carried on with what she had been doing.

It was just around half past three when her intercom went. 'Come in, Emily, please,' her employer instructed.

Certainly, your libertine-ness! Without a word Emmie picked up her pad and went in. And for the next half an hour she took dictation or jotted down his instructions. She was still writing when the phone in her office rang.

Cunningham indicated she should stay where she was, and, reaching for the phone on his desk, pressed the appropriate button. 'Cunningham,' he said, and then there was a smile there in his voice as his caller announced herself. 'Roberta! You cunning vixen, how's it going?' he asked.

Emmie didn't like it. A kind of sickness hit her, and she wanted to dash out of there. She made to leave—she could come back later, when he'd finished chatting up the 'cunning vixen'. Cunning, no doubt, because she was successfully fooling her husband! But Barden Cunningham motioned her to sit down again. All too obviously he didn't give a damn that Emmie overheard his philandering phone calls. Why couldn't he conduct his wretched affair outside business hours?

She had no idea what Roberta's replies were, but what Cunningham was saying didn't leave Emmie in very much doubt that the conclusions she'd drawn were correct.

'You're worrying too much!' Cunningham teased. 'I promise you he's not likely to divorce you.'

Grief—how was that for confident! Even if Neville Short did find out about the affair, the poor chap so loved his wife he would never divorce her. Barden Cunningham was taking advantage of that! Locking up! He should be put down—preferably painfully! The call was coming to an end.

'I'll somehow manage to snatch a few moments with you tomorrow night at the theatre,' Barden promised. 'It shouldn't be too difficult.'

There was a pause as Roberta replied—and Emmie started to get angry. She knew full well that it was nothing to do with her, but, confound it! Not content to play fast and loose behind the cuckolded Neville's back, it sounded very much as though Cunningham would be seeing them both at the theatre tomorrow, and—given half a chance—he would snatch his opportunity for a quick cuddle right under her husband's—*his friend's*—nose. Oh, it was too much!

'You've nothing to worry about. I promise you, Neville

has no idea what you're up to,' Barden soothed. 'Now stop worrying. I'll see you tomorrow. Everything will be fine.'

She'd bet it would, Emmie fumed. Quite plainly Roberta Short was getting the wind up that her poor husband might find out what was going on. And Barden Cunningham, who was no doubt no stranger to this sort of situation, was almost casual as he attempted to soothe Roberta's anxieties.

'Now what did I do?'

The tone was sharp. Emmie looked up—he had ended his phone call, though she would have known that from his tone of voice, which was oh, so very different from how it had been now that he was no longer speaking to his lady-love.

Emmie strove hard to keep a lid on her anger. 'Do?' she countered.

'I've just about had it with you and your arrogance!' Barden Cunningham snarled curtly. Arrogance? Her? Emmie could feel herself fighting a losing battle with her anger, even if she was desperate to keep her job. She sensed from his statement, 'I've just about had it with you', that she was on her way out, anyway. 'So tell me what I did this time.' He gave her a direct look from those no-nonsense cool grey eyes, and Emmie just knew that he was going to pursue this until he had an answer.

'It's none of my business.' She felt forced, if she hoped to hang on to this job, to give him some sort of a reply.

'What isn't?'

As she'd thought. He wanted more than that. 'When Mrs Short rang earlier she was very anxious that her husband didn't know about it.'

'So!'

Oh, abomination, he was immovable. 'Add that to the conversation—well, your side anyway, which I've just overheard—and it's obvious!'

'What is?'

She wanted to hit him. He wanted her to come right out

with it. Well, she'd be damned if she would. 'If you don't know, it's not up to me to tell you!' She could feel her temper getting away from her. Cool it, cool it, you can't afford a temper.

'You think—' He broke off, and, putting her remark about Mrs Short being anxious about her husband knowing, together with the exchange he'd just had with her, he suddenly had it all added up. 'How d—?' He was angry; she could tell. That made two of them. 'Why, you prissy little Miss Prim and Proper. You think I'm having an affair with—'

'It's nothing to do with me!' Emmie flared. Her on-the-loose temper had no chance while that 'prissy little Miss Prim and Proper' still floated in the air.

'You're damned right it isn't!' he barked. He was on his feet—so was she. 'What I do with my life, how I conduct my life, is absolutely, categorically, nothing whatsoever to do with you!' he snarled. *'Got that?'*

Who did he think he was? Who did he think he was talking to? Some mealy-mouthed, wouldn't-say-boo typist? 'It was you who insisted on knowing!' she erupted, her brown eyes sparking flashes of fire.

She refused to back down, even though she knew he was going to well and truly attempt to sort her out now. Strangely, though, as she waited for him to rain coals of wrath down about her head, all at once, as he looked into her storming brown eyes, it seemed he checked himself—and decided to sort her out using another tack. For suddenly his tone became more mocking than angry.

'Are you being fair, do you think, little Emily?' he enquired charmingly.

She blinked. 'Fair?' She owned she wasn't quite with him.

'I don't—scold—you over your affairs,' he drawled, and she looked at him, momentarily made speechless. 'But then,' he went on coolly, 'you've never had an affair, have you?'

She hadn't. But pride, some kind of inverted honour, was at stake here. 'I've…' she began, ready to lie and tell him she'd had dozens of affairs—only she faltered. Given that it seemed it was she who had instigated this conversation, was she really discussing her love-life—or his view that she didn't *have* a love life—with her employer? 'How many affairs I've had, or not had, is entirely nothing to do with you,' she jumped back up on her high horse, and told him loftily.

'Typical!' he rapped, soon back to snarling, she noted. 'You think you can pass judgement on my out-of-work activities, but the moment I enquire into yours, it's none of my business!'

'Out-of-work activities'. That was a new name for it! But she'd had enough, and grabbed up her notepad. 'Do you want this work back today or don't you?' she challenged hotly—and too late saw the glint in his eyes that clearly said he didn't take very kindly to attitude.

Oddly again, though—when some part of her already wanted to apologise, while another part wouldn't let her—instead of laying into her, as she'd fully expected, Barden Cunningham took a moment out to look down at her. She knew from her burning skin that she must have flares of pink in her cheeks. She was, however, already regretting her spurt of temper, and on the way to vowing never to get angry again, when still looking down at her, that glint of anger in those no-nonsense grey eyes suddenly became a mocking glint as he derided, 'And there was I, putting you down as a mouse.'

That did it! Mouse! Apologise? She'd see him hang first! Mouse! What self-respecting twenty-two-year-old would put up with that? 'Better a mouse than a *rat*!' she hissed—and was on her way.

She went storming through the connecting door, not

bothering to close it—she wasn't stopping—and straight to her coat peg on the far wall. Even as she reached for her coat, though, and started shrugging into it, she was regretting having lost her temper. What the dickens was the matter with her? She couldn't afford a temper!

Emmie dipped in the bottom drawer of her desk to retrieve her bag, knowing full well that even if she didn't want to go there was no way now, after calling Barden Cunningham a rat, that he was going to let her stay.

Or so she'd thought. She had just straightened, her shoulder bag in hand, when his voice enquired coolly, 'Where do you think you're going?'

She looked over to the doorway and saw he had come to lean nonchalantly against the doorframe. She hesitated, common practical sense intruding on what pride decreed. Oh, she did so like the work, and didn't want to leave. Her breath caught. Was he saying that, despite her poking her nose into his private life and making judgements on his morals, he wasn't telling her to go?

'Aren't I—dismissed?' she managed to query.

For answer Barden Cunningham stood away from the door. 'I'll let you know when,' he drawled—and added, with insincere charm, 'You'll be working late tonight.'

With that he went into his office, and, obviously utterly confident that she would do exactly as he said, and not bothering to wait to see if she took her coat off, closed the connecting door.

Emmie slowly put down her bag, relief rushing in because she still had this well-paid and, it had to be said, enjoyable job—while another part of her, the proud part, she rather suspected, made her wish she was in a position to walk and keep on walking.

A cold war ensued for the remainder of the day.

Working late was of no concern to Emmie, and she arrived at her flat around eight that evening, starting to feel quite astonished that, though her security was so vital to her, she had today, because she had been unable to control a suddenly erratic temper, put both her security and Aunt Hannah's future tranquillity at risk!

Emmie got up the following morning, still wondering what in creation had got into her. She was aware that she had been tremendously shaken when her stepfather Alec had died. Her emotions had received a terrible blow. Her redundancy from Usher Trading around about the same time hadn't helped. The worrying time she'd had of it when each of her successive jobs had folded had been a strain too. Had she perhaps grown too used to heading for the door when something went wrong, and had it become a habit with her?

But, not without cause, she mused as she drove to the offices of Progress Engineering. She remembered Clive Norris's attempt to kiss her. The way he'd hemmed her in between the filing cabinet and the wall—was she supposed to put up with that sort of nonsense? No, certainly not!

So what had Cunningham done that had made her so angry? So angry that for emotional seconds at a time she had been ready to forget her oh, so important security and walk out of there. Made him so angry she had thought herself about to be dismissed at any second—thought she *had* really blown it when she'd more or less called him a rat.

So he was, too. But was it any of her business? She hadn't liked it when he'd said he thought of her as a mouse. Nor had she liked it when he'd referred to her non-existent love-life. But, and Emmie had to face it, she was employed by Barden Cunningham to work, and only work. *She* had been the one to bring the personal element into it. True, the whole sorry business could have been avoided if he hadn't enquired so sharply—in such a direct contrast to his tone when talking to his lady-love, Roberta Short—'Now what did I do?'

Or could it have been avoided? He'd caught her on the

raw with his tone, and negated any chance of her making use of the skills of diplomacy she'd assured him at her interview she possessed, without those sharp words telling her he'd just about had it with her and her arrogance. And, if that hadn't been enough, he'd insisted on knowing why she was being 'arrogant' this time.

Emmie went to her desk, aware by then that she was at fault. Anything that happened in the office that wasn't business was nothing to do with her. Unless the womanising hound made a pass at her—and she could be part of the furniture for all the notice he took of her; not that she wanted him taking notice of her, thank you very much—perish the thought. But she had no call to be remotely interested in anything else that went on which was unconnected with business.

'Everything all right?' she asked Dawn after their initial greeting.

'As it should be.' Dawn smiled.

'How are you feeling today?'

'Touch wood, so far, and in comparison to Tuesday, quite good.'

Emmie got on with some work, but the row she'd had with Barden Cunningham the previous afternoon came back again and again to haunt her. Somehow, when at around eleven he called her into his office, she knew that she was not going to forget it, or indeed feel any better about it, until she'd apologised.

But he was cool, aloof, as he stated, 'I have to go to Stratford—be ready at twelve.'

She felt niggled; no please, no thank you, no Could you be ready at twelve; I'd like you to accompany me? The cold war was still on, then? He was charm personified with everyone else.

'Will you require any file in particular?' she enquired politely, knowing by then that they had a product and design offshoot in Stratford-upon-Avon, about a hundred and ten miles away.

'Just a fresh notebook,' he replied. 'You're taking the minutes of what could be a lengthy, involved and very important meeting.'

Emmie returned to her desk, glad she was wearing the same smart charcoal suit she had worn for her interview. She knew she was looking good, and felt it was quite a feather in her cap that she had been appointed to go with the head of the group to take notes for this very important meeting. Although, on thinking about it, she had known from the first that Dawn wasn't able to go. Barden could easily have found someone else, though. Emmie cheered herself up. Make no mistake, please or offend, he would have found someone else if he thought for a moment that she wasn't up to it.

They made it to Stratford-upon-Avon in good time, and were greeted by the general manager, Jack Bryant, a pleasant man in his early thirties who, while totally businesslike with her employer, frequently rested his eyes on Emmie.

'I refuse to believe you're called Emily,' he commented, while Barden was having a word with the products manager.

'Would you believe Emmie?'

He smiled, and when Emmie was starting to wonder if she was going to last the whole afternoon, lunchless, he informed her, 'A meal's been laid on for you in the executive dining room.' He was just adding, 'I hope you won't mind if I have lunch with you too, Emmie,' when she became aware that Barden Cunningham had turned back to them.

He tossed her a sour look, which she took as an indication that he felt she hadn't wasted any time in giving the general manager leave to call her by the name all but he used. Then he looked from her to remark, a touch sarcastically, she felt, 'Good of you to wait lunch.'

They did not linger over the meal, and, having been given all of five minutes to wash her hands afterwards, they adjourned to the boardroom and the afternoon flew as fast as her fingers. Emmie had known she was good at her job, but at that meeting her skills were tested to the full. When it came to an end she felt as if she had done a full week's work in one afternoon.

Jack Bryant came over to her while Barden was shaking hands with a couple of the board members. 'I'm in London quite often, or could be.' Jack smiled. 'You wouldn't care to let me have your phone number, I suppose?'

'Your divorce through yet, Jack?' Barden appeared from nowhere to ask conversationally.

'Any time now,' he replied.

Barden smiled. 'Talk to my PA when it's absolute—she doesn't encourage married men.'

Why did she want to hit him? On the one hand she was thrilled to bits that he'd actually called her his PA, but on the other she wanted to land him one. For all it was true, and she didn't encourage married men, he somehow made it sound as if she really was the 'prissy little Miss Prim and Proper' he had called her yesterday. That still stung!

It was around seven-thirty when they arrived back at the Progress Engineering building, and by then the mixed feelings about her employer Emmie had been experiencing had calmed down, to the extent that she was again thinking of the apology she owed him.

Intending to lock her notes away in her desk overnight, Emmie went up to her office in the lift with Barden, and he took a short cut through her office to his own. Placing her bag and pad down on her desk, she heard him at his desk, and, acting on the impulse of the moment—and in a now-or-never attempt to get her apology over and done with—she went and paused in the doorway.

Barden Cunningham looked over to where she stood— and her words wouldn't come. He waited, his glance taking in her straight and shiny black hair, flicking over her suit, which concealed her slender figure. Unspeaking, his glance came back to her face, to her eyes, down to her mouth, where the words trembled, and then back up to her eyes.

Emmie knew then that if she didn't push those words out soon she was going to lose all dignity and feel a fool. 'I—I want to apologise for my—er—behaviour yesterday,' she forced out jerkily—and wished she hadn't bothered when, instantly aware of what she was referring to, but not looking at all friendly, he looked coolly back at her.

'You're still of the same view today as yesterday?' he enquired crisply.

The view that he was a rat for playing away with Neville Short's wife while pretending to be his good friend? Yes, she did still hold the same view. Why couldn't Cunningham just accept her apology and forget it? But—he was waiting, and Emmie just then discovered that, even though a lie, a simple no would have ended the matter, suddenly, lying was beyond her.

'Yes,' she said quietly, weathering the direct look from those no-nonsense steady grey eyes. 'My views haven't changed.'

The no-nonsense look went from cool to icy. 'Then your apology is worthless,' he stated curtly.

Emmie abruptly turned her back on him and marched stormily into her own office. She didn't know about losing dignity, but she did feel a fool—and humiliated into the bargain. Heartily did she wish she had never bothered, had ignored the plague of her conscience. Her apology was rejected. Huh! The way he talked, he would only accept her apology if it was sincere. *He* was so sincere! Stabbing his friend Neville in the back—it looked like it!

Fuming, Emmie tossed her notepad in her drawer and locked it away—only to feel like storming in and punching Barden Cunningham's head when his voice floated coolly from his office. 'Leave typing back your notes until the morning, Emily.'

Was he serious? He actually thought she had it in mind to type up those minutes *tonight*? There was a full day's work there! Resisting the temptation to go to his doorway and poke her tongue out at him, Emmie instead picked up her bag and went swiftly to her outer office door.

Afraid that if she opened her mouth something not very polite would come out, she decided against wishing him goodnight, but, by switching out the light and plunging her office in darkness, she let that be her farewell to him. The swine. He had an assignation with Roberta Short at the theatre that night. He must already be late—she hoped that he wouldn't be let in.

Emmie had difficulty in getting to sleep that night. It seemed to her that she only had to close her eyes to start wondering if Cunningham had managed to snatch some private time with his married lover. Perhaps even now, at this very moment, they were alone together. The thought made her feel quite wretched. She moved and thumped her pillow—wishing that it was his head.

She surfaced on Friday, after a very fractured night, and showered and donned a white silk shirt and her second-best suit of dark navy wool. Satisfied with her appearance, and aware that, since her notes from yesterday needed to be typed up she was in for a hard day, she was about to don her three-quarter-length car coat when her phone rang.

Aunt Hannah? She didn't normally ring in the morning on a weekday. Though since she did sometimes get her days mixed up, which was perfectly understandable, Emmie defended, perhaps Aunt Hannah thought today was Saturday.

Emmie went over to the phone, checking her watch and mentally noting she had five minutes to spare if it was Aunt Hannah.

The call *was* from Keswick House, she soon discovered.

However, it was not her step-grandmother—but Lisa Browne. Mrs Whitford was not to be found, and enquiries had revealed that one of the other residents had seen her letting herself out an hour ago. She hadn't told anyone where she was going.

An hour ago! Aunt Hannah didn't usually get up this early! Emmie took a quick glance to the window, trying not to panic. It was a grey day; snow was threatening. 'Was she wearing a coat?' she asked quickly.

'Apparently, yes.'

'She's probably gone back to our old apartment.' Emmie spoke her thoughts out loud, panic mixing with concern that Aunt Hannah might be getting confused again. 'I'll go there straight away,' she told Lisa Browne—and wasted no more time.

Only when the cold air hit her did it vaguely dawn on her that she had rushed out without actually putting her own coat on. But she had more important matters to worry about than that—she'd soon get warm in the car. She must get the car heated up for Aunt Hannah. Must collect her. Must return her to Keswick House. Must get to work. Oh, heck, all that work she had to do today! Barden Cunningham was just going to love her. She tried not to think about him. This was the last day of her fifth week at Progress—and the first time she'd been late.

Hoping that her five-week record for being on time, not to mention that she had uncomplainingly worked late when required, would see her employer—womanising toad—forgiving her this one lapse—she couldn't bear to think that there might be another—Emmie concentrated on her most immediate problem. Her present accommodation was just five miles away from Keswick House; the apartment where they'd used to live was seven miles distant from Aunt Hannah's new home. For someone so confused that she had in the past believed that she still lived in their old apartment, it was a source of surprise to Emmie that, even in the depths of confusion, Aunt Hannah remembered their previous address and how to get there.

Thinking she would soon have her step-relative safe in her car, Emmie was delayed by twenty minutes in traffic. When eventually she did make it to the area where she had lived happily with Alec and his mother, Emmie looked about for signs of the dear love.

With not a glimpse of her, she parked outside her old address and rang the doorbells of their former neighbours. No one answered. For the next hour Emmie scoured the streets, looking for Aunt Hannah. Starting to feel quite desperate, she went back to her present flat, hoping that Aunt Hannah had thought to go there.

She hadn't. Emmie rang Lisa Browne, crossing her fingers that her step-relative had made it back to Keswick House. 'I'm afraid not,' Lisa Browne answered.

By then Emmie was getting seriously worried. She thought of ringing the police, then decided she would give it one more try. Aunt Hannah had grown aggressive the last time she'd been in police 'custody'.

Emmie did also consider ringing Dawn at Progress Engineering, but, as distracted as Emmie felt, she remembered just in time how Barden Cunningham had specifically asked her at her interview if she had any commitments. She had an idea she was going to be in enough trouble when she did eventually reach her office without now confessing that she had lied at her interview.

Emmie was back on the road to her old home once more when it came to her that because of her lie about no commitments she would be unable to tell the truth. She suddenly realised she had no excuse to offer for her absence!

All that, however, went from her mind when, just as she reached their former apartment, she saw Aunt Hannah getting out of a delivery van. The van drove off. Emmie made it to the pavement just as Mrs Whitford was about to climb the steps to the front door.

'Aunt Hannah!' she called, loud enough for her to hear, but not enough to startle the old lady.

Aunt Hannah turned and, seeing Emmie, smiled. 'Hello, dear. Not at work today? I waited ages for a bus, but that driver stopped and—' She broke off, something of much greater importance occurring to her. 'Do you know, he used to have a Norton 16H too?'

Emmie smiled; her relief at having found Hannah was enormous! The dear love was motorbike crazy, and, in her unconventional younger years, had owned several machines. 'How are you?' Emmie enquired, as a precursor to getting her in the car and driving her back to Keswick House.

'Oh, very well. Mr Norton,' she went on, making Emmie smile—the van driver and ex-motorbike owner was obviously Mr Norton!—'was telling me about the National Motorcycle Museum in Birmingham. It's open seven days a week,' she hinted.

How could you not love her? Emmie smiled fondly. 'We'll go,' she promised. 'Not today,' she added quickly, 'but soon. It must be getting near to your lunchtime. Shall we go back to Keswick House?'

It was closer to twelve than eleven by the time Emmie had got Aunt Hannah cheerfully settled back at Keswick House, and nearer one than twelve when she made it to her office. She noted that Dawn wasn't around when she went in, and stowed her bag, glad that the door between her office and the next one was closed.

It did not stay closed for long. Trust *him* to have heard her. Barden Cunningham pulled back the door and took a pace into the room, his glance becoming more and more hostile the longer he looked at her. She swallowed. Oh, crumbs, it looked like fire and brimstone time!

It was. He took a long breath, as if needing control, 'Since you obviously haven't been rushed to hospital to have your appendix removed,' he began, silkily enough—

it didn't last. 'Would you mind telling me,' he went on toughly, 'just where the hell you've been?'

'I—er—had a domestic problem.' Emmie found her voice, hoping he would think her central heating system had malfunctioned.

'Don't tell me you've broken the habit of a lifetime and let some man into your bed!' he snarled, his idea of domesticity clearly on a very different plane from hers.

The cheek of it! 'According to you, I don't have an overnight life!' Emmie flared, not at all enamoured by his snarling sarcastic tone, but striving hard not to let it get to her.

'What was this ''domestic'' matter?' he went on, as if he hadn't heard her. 'Couldn't you get him to leave?'

Emmie lost it. 'Don't judge me by your own criteria!' she flew. Oh, grief, he looked ready to throttle her. All too obviously he hadn't cared for that. She wanted to back down, wanted to regret her words—but she found she couldn't. Oh, what was the matter with her? She had pushed her luck yesterday, and the day before—she couldn't hope to be so lucky again, and she needed this job! 'Er—has Dawn gone for an early lunch?' She attempted to cool both her temper and his. Fat chance!

'I've given her the day off!' he gritted. 'When *she*, despite how off-colour she's feeling, managed to get to a phone—' sarcastic swine! '—I decided we'd cope without her.'

Bully for you! Emmie, hoping, since she was still there, that she hadn't received her marching orders, offered, 'I'll make up my time off. I'll work late tonight and—'

'You're damned right you will,' Barden cut in bluntly. 'I want those minutes finished and in my hands before this day is over!'

Emmie stared at him. He *had* to be joking! Pride—she guessed that was what it was—wouldn't allow her to tell him she couldn't do it. She was supposed to be cooking a meal for Adrian Payne that night. 'Do I take it that you'll be staying late too?' she enquired, as evenly as she could.

He smiled then, an insincere smile. And she, who had never hated anyone in her life, well and truly hated Barden Cunningham then. She hated him particularly when, his tone again silky, he replied, 'No way. I was here before seven this morning. I'm just about to leave for a weekend party.'

Fuming, while trying to hold her temper down, Emmie stared belligerently at him. 'You're saying that you want me to cancel my date tonight, to work until I'm ready to drop, in order to lock those minutes away in a drawer for your attention on Monday?'

He didn't smile, but his tone stayed pleasant as he admonished, 'You weren't listening, Emily. I said I want those completed minutes *in my hands today*.'

'But—but you're going—er—partying!'

'True,' he answered, and, reaching for a sheet of office stationery, swiftly wrote down an address and some directions. 'I don't doubt the party will still be thrashing gone midnight. I'm sure you won't mind dropping off the minutes on your way home.'

Emmie took the paper from him and stared at it. Then, her eyes widening, she stared at him. The address—Neville and Roberta Short's address—lay in an entirely different direction from where she lived. And she was positive the vile Cunningham *knew* it! She flicked her glance past him to the window, where the first flakes of snow had started to fall. A glance back at her employer showed he'd followed her eyes.

He looked back to her—and smiled. Then she hated him afresh! He knew full well that she would be slaving away until at least eight o'clock that night. And after that it would take her an hour to drive to his *lady-love's* home!

She opened her mouth to protest, then all at once realised from his silky look that it was just what he was expecting—

and she knew she'd see him in hell first! She swallowed down all hint of protest. 'Anything else?' she enquired prettily—and thought she caught a glimpse of something akin to admiration in his eyes.

It was gone in an instant, and she knew that she must have imagined it when he went to the door. Though, once there, he turned, and his agreeable tone beat hers by a mile when he reminded her, 'Don't forget to break your date, Emily,' and went off for his evil weekend. Emmie actually thought she heard him whistling as he went!

CHAPTER THREE

BY GOING without a lunchtime and working as fast as she could, though telephone interruptions caused her to stop all too often, Emmie completed her work just after eight that evening. She felt drained and exhausted, but also triumphant.

She also felt extremely anti Mr Barden-womanising-Cunningham. She hated him, and hated that he was actually spending a partying weekend in his married lover's *home*. How *could* he?

Emmie, still winter coat-less, dashed from her office to her car, glad to note that there wasn't too much snow around. She started the engine and headed the vehicle in the direction of Neville and Roberta Short's home, making herself calm down. For goodness' sake, it was nothing to do with her what Cunningham did in his spare time.

She drove on, realising, since her security was so important to her, she should count herself lucky that after her non-attendance this morning she still had a job. A well-paid job, too.

All thoughts, however, of how grateful she should be that she had kept her job began to disappear from her mind when, clear of London, she started to drive into bad weather. It started snowing again. It will stop soon, she told herself, just as her stomach began to violently protest because, apart from breakfast, it hadn't been fed that day. The snow kept falling.

After quite some while she saw a signpost, fortunately not yet obscured by snow, which showed that her destination was not so far distant. Emmie turned off the major road she was on and steered down a minor one.

By then food was starting to dominate. She had phoned Adrian and cancelled their meal, but felt hungry enough to eat a dry bread sandwich. She was aware that if she didn't stop now and have something to eat she might well be unlucky on the way back, if any pub she came across stopped serving food at nine-thirty.

She was almost at a pub when she knew she *must* eat something before she got home. For heaven's sake, she started to fume, *he'd* be so busy partying he was never going to notice what time she got to the Shorts'—and she was *starving*! Telling herself that, provided those minutes were in Barden's hands by midnight, it would still count as *today*, just like he had ordered—though of course she'd be handing them over well before then—within the next hour if the service in The Farmer's Arms was pretty smart—Emmie turned into the pub car park.

The service was not swift, and it seemed to take for ever for the prawn risotto she had ordered to arrive, though it was nicely presented, with a couple of decorative prawns on the side.

The taste left something to be desired, but Emmie was by then ravenous, and the risotto was filling. She felt much more cheerful as she made to leave the pub than when she had entered it.

Any feeling of cheerfulness abruptly vanished, however, when she opened the door to the outside elements. It was snowing a blizzard out there! Already the roads were well covered. Snowflakes as big as buckets charged straight for her.

The winter chill bit through the thin wool of her suit as, taking her life in her hands—in her two-and-a-half-inch heels—Emmie hurried over the snow-covered ground to her car. She turned the key in the ignition and saw from the clock that it was already half past nine. She just couldn't believe it!

According to her calculations at the outset, she should

have been back at her own home about ten-thirtyish. Well, she could forget that! She wished she could forget having to go to the Shorts' house. But she wanted this job, and *he* was a pig, and the sooner she got there the sooner she'd get back. By her reckoning, and with a fair wind, she would be heading back in little over half an hour.

Matters did not work out as planned. Her initial estimate had been that it would take around an hour for her to complete the distance to the Shorts' home. But she found that she was out by thirty minutes—and that would have been in normal weather conditions.

With the wind howling, the snow falling thick and fast and coming straight at her, visibility was next to nil. Having no wish to end up in a ditch, Emmie slowed her speed to a crawl. She was not happy. She felt isolated, alone, and very sorely tempted to give in to the instinct to turn around and head for home.

Doggedly, she pressed on, reminding herself again and again that *he* wanted those minutes, but, more importantly than that, she wanted, nay, needed quite desperately to keep this job.

Feeling both mentally and physically exhausted, while mutinying that she must be the only driver out on a night like this, for she hadn't seen so much as a glimpse of another vehicle since she had driven away from The Farmer's Arms, Emmie experienced a tremendous uplift of spirits when she found she had arrived at the edge of the village she was looking for.

She relaxed her concentration for the briefest of moments—it was a mistake. The worst happened. She skidded off the road down a gully and into a hedge. Her car, she knew instantly, was going no further. She tried anyway, put it into reverse and gently accelerated—but her wheels spun.

Emmie tried for the next ten minutes. Even while knowing it was hopeless she tried. It was going to take a tractor to pull her out. She glanced about, but couldn't see very much. But, though she didn't fancy at all getting out of her car—she'd freeze out there—common sense alerted that if she stayed in her car all night it was a near certainty she'd freeze to death anyway.

Grabbing up the minutes folder from the passenger seat, Emmie, with some difficulty, because of the angle of her car, managed to open her door sufficiently to be able to squeeze out.

Cold air hit her. Scrambling up the small incline, she fell over and measured her length. She scrabbled to her feet— her shoes were never going to be the same again—and started walking towards a distant glimmer of light.

Slithering and sliding on her smart shoes to what she saw now was a streetlamp, Emmie fell over once more in the ankle-deep snow before she reached the lamp. Then she saw a signpost and went to brush snow from it—and so get her bearings. The Shorts' home was on the outskirts of the village. Her good fortune was that she had 'parked' her car at the right end. If she took a left turn, the Shorts' place should be a hundred or so yards in that direction.

Mutiny entered Emmie's soul as she trudged, slithered and slid, and getting wetter by the second, doggedly ploughed on. *He* wanted the minutes; she'd give him the minutes! What did he want them for anyway during his partying weekend? Was he expecting there to be a dull moment or two? She hoped so.

She hoped it was the dullest weekend that he had ever spent. She hoped that Neville Short found out that Cunningham was having an affair with his wife and that Neville beat the hell out of him. Though, recalling Neville's gentle manner and average build, she supposed he'd have a bit of a job giving the taller, fitter-looking Cunningham a pasting.

Why didn't the Shorts have a fax machine anyway? Emmie fell over again, and got up feeling soaked to her skin—and fuming—but not defeated. If only she didn't need this rotten, stinking, foul pig of a job, given to her by that pig of a man… Calling him all the worst names she could think of got her through the last fifty yards. She trudged on—then saw it. A dim light at first, and then bit by tiny bit, as she drew closer, more light, in fact a whole house with all lights blazing.

She felt ready to drop as she went achingly up the drive, passing snow-covered parked cars—and wanted only her bed. She felt too tired even to think of what would happen once she'd handed over the by now soggy folder she had come to deliver.

Emmie struggled up the steps, and with fingers numb with cold managed to ring the bell. She could hear laughter and music going on inside—she wanted to sleep. The door opened. She recognised an astonished Roberta Short, the last word in elegance. Snow billowed into the beautifully carpeted hall.

'Come in, come in,' Roberta beckoned urgently. Emmie needed no further urging. It was only then, though, that she realised what a sight she must look, when Roberta peered into her face and, obviously having not recognised her but clearly being of such a charitable nature that she would not have left anyone standing on the doorstep on a night like this, exclaimed, 'Why, it's Emmie, isn't it? Barden's Emmie.'

Emmie was by then too fatigued to argue that she was neither Barden's Emmie nor anyone else's. But just then, as if his name being mentioned had conjured him up, Barden Cunningham appeared.

Dressed in crisp white shirt, and dinner-suited, he had never looked so handsome—nor so astounded. 'You… What are you doing here?' he asked—and if she'd had the energy Emmie was certain she would have set about him.

'You wanted these minutes!' she stated belligerently.

'You haven't driven out on a night like this purely to—' He broke off, plainly not crediting the evidence of his own eyes. 'Only an idiot would...' he was going on, when abruptly he changed his mind, and turned to Roberta. 'May we use the library?' he asked.

Emmie no more cared for being called an idiot than she cared to go to the library with him. But she had nowhere else just then that she particularly wanted to go. Though in any case he was taking a hold of her arm and...

'You're soaking!' he exclaimed.

'So would you be if you'd just walked ten miles.' She might be dead on her feet but discovered that there was still some life in her yet.

'You've walked ten miles—in this weather!'

No wonder he was incredulous. 'Superwoman I'm not! My car skidded into a hedge down the road and won't budge—the walk just seemed like ten miles.'

'Are you hurt?'

They were passing a hall mirror. She halted; her escort halted too. 'Is that me?' she asked croakily of the wreck with bedraggled, dripping hair and blue with cold that stared back at her.

Barden Cunningham did not answer her question, but repeated, 'Are you hurt anywhere?'

She stared, still disbelieving of her reflection. 'Just my pride,' she muttered miserably. But liked him when for a short moment he smiled gently at her in the mirror.

'I'm sure no one ever had such a loyal and trustworthy personal assistant,' he murmured, and moved her away from the mirror, taking her to the library and closing the door. He kept a hold of her arm as he switched on an electric fire. 'Stand there for a minute,' he instructed, 'I won't be long.'

With that he left her, and Emmie went closer to the fire, her teeth chattering as she stretched out her hands, hoping that some part of her would soon be warm. True to his word, Barden was not away long. He returned carrying towels and a towelling robe.

'Roberta wanted to come and look after you herself, but this is a special party for her husband. I told her you wouldn't mind putting up with me.' He smiled.

Emmie had never expected to be on the receiving end of his charm—she wasn't sure how she felt about it. 'I can look after myself,' she told him grumpily.

'I'm sure you can,' he soothed. 'But I'm your boss—humour me.' Her teeth started chattering again—and the teasing was over. 'Right,' he declared authoritatively. 'Get out of your wet clothes, rub yourself dry, and put that robe on.'

She wanted to argue, but didn't have the energy. To get out of her wet clothes seemed, just then, to be the best idea she'd heard in a long while. She raised her frozen hands to the buttons of her jacket, but her fingers were so cold, the material so wet, she couldn't undo so much as one.

Barden saw her plight and without fuss, without bother, came and stood in front of her. With deft fingers he undid her jacket and helped her out of it. He placed it on the floor and returned, raising his hands to the clinging dampness of her silk shirt.

'I—can…' she said quickly. But found she couldn't.

She felt she liked him a little bit more when, seeing the dreadful time her numbed fingers were having, he came forward again and almost tenderly murmured, 'I think I know that you're not used to men undressing you, little Emmie, but—I'm special.'

Somehow, though she had a kind of woolly feeling that all this was happening to someone else and not her, Emmie managed to find a bit of a smile—that was the first time he had ever called her Emmie! 'If you could just undo the fastenings, I can manage the rest.'

His answer was to raise his hands near her bosom and efficiently undo the tiny buttons of her silk shirt. Before she could make further protest, though for the moment she was feeling too defeated to say anything very much at all,

Barden made a workman-like job of unzipping her skirt. 'Anything else you need a hand with?' he enquired, his tone somehow impersonal, given that she knew he meant her only other problem: her bra fastening. She stepped back, shaking her head, and found his eyes on her eyes. But he accepted her refusal, and instructed, 'As quick as you can, then, out of your clothes, rub yourself dry and get into the robe.'

Emmie, not moving, continued to stare at him—and felt strangely weepy when those grey eyes which she was more used to seeing with chips of ice in them suddenly seemed warm as he smiled the gentlest of smiles.

'You're a rare one, Emily Lawson,' he said quietly—and turned and left her.

Emmie stared after him for a few moments. Was this man with the gentle way the same pig of a man she worked for? Her skirt started to steam. She moved six inches away from the fire and, suddenly afraid someone might come in and catch her naked, undressed as fast as she was able, opting to stay with her briefs and bra.

She found she didn't have the energy to give herself much of a rubbing, but did what she could, and rubbed at her hair. Shortly afterwards, wrapped in an over-large white towelling robe, and with a big white towel around her head, Emmie was starting to recover. She still felt very tired, but her brain, which had seemed as numbed by the wet and cold as the rest of her, was starting to come out of hibernation.

Sounds of a riotous party going on elsewhere in the house reached her as, seated on the carpet, she toasted herself by the fire. Emmie started to wonder if perhaps Roberta Short would lend her some of her old clothes. Although, remembering Roberta's elegance, Emmie doubted that she had any 'old' clothes.

The door behind her suddenly opened, and a gust of

laughter came in before the door was closed again. Emmie jerked round and saw her employer.

'Soup,' he explained about the mug he was carrying on a tray. 'You can thaw your insides with it while we talk.'

Talk? What was there to talk about? 'You're not intending to give me dictation, I hope?' She made to get up, but he motioned that she should stay where she was.

He handed her the soup, 'I see you've got your sauce back,' he commented mildly as he pulled round a padded chair and sat close by. 'Have you had any dinner?'

'I had a bite of something on the way. I didn't know then that the weather was going to be so bad,' she quickly excused. 'I'm—er—feeling warmer,' she added.

'Good. Drink your soup.'

He was back to being bossy. She didn't like him again. Absurdly, she felt she wanted him back being gentle. Abruptly she pulled herself together. Grief, the snow must have addled her brain!

'I'm sorry I've—er—been such a nuisance,' she apologised. Then truly got herself together. 'Only you did definitely say you wanted these minutes in your hands today.'

'It hadn't occurred to me you'd put your life at risk to deliver them,' he replied coolly.

'I only went off the road—I got out of my car in one piece!' she retorted sniffily, not caring in the least for his tone.

'A car that's going nowhere,' he stated, and added bluntly, 'And neither are you.'

She wanted to argue. Her frozen spirits had revived. She wanted to tell him that she wasn't at work now, so he could keep his bossy opinions to himself. But he'd said she was going nowhere and—since her car was stuck fast—what alternative did she have? If she said, as she felt like saying, that she was leaving she would confirm his previous opinion that only an idiot would be out on a night like this.

And, truth to tell, the idea of going out again in those night-marish elements while it was still dark was quite terrifying.

That didn't stop her from feeling mutinous, though, as she stared at Barden Cunningham and enquired snappily, 'You're suggesting I find myself a corner somewhere until morning?'

'We can do better than that,' he answered crisply. 'Though, as you can imagine, no one with any sense is driving very far tonight.' Rub it in! 'So, while Roberta and Neville's guests who have four-wheeled-drive vehicles will be returning to their homes in due time, others who hadn't planned to stay will be. As...' he paused '...will you.'

'Make me feel good, why don't you!' Oh, this was intolerable. 'I'm sorry,' she apologised. What in creation was the matter with her? She was feeling weepy again. 'I—I didn't mean to disrupt the whole household. I'll find a sofa somewhere and...'

'In case you hadn't noticed, there's a party going on,' he reminded her. 'A party you're welcome to join, but by the look of you I'd say you're too exhausted for anything but sleep.'

'I don't suppose I would get much sleep in the drawing room,' she answered, knowing full well that he was meaning that no one would want to party round a recumbent robe-clad female dossing down on the party room sofa.

He smiled then. It seemed to work some magic. Emmie found that she was smiling too. She was not smiling for long, however, and nor was he when he stated matter-of-factly, 'The situation is this: all the spare bedrooms have been taken, but...'

'But?' she questioned, somehow instinct telling her that she wasn't going to care very much for that 'but'.

'But there is a spare bed going.'

'Oh, yes?' she answered, feeling wary without knowing why. 'I'm not going to like this, am I?'

'You haven't very much choice,' he replied, and without

more ado announced, 'The spare bed happens to be in the room I'm using.'

'No way!'

'You can always go outside and try to hitch a lift home!' he rapped shortly.

'I didn't see one single solitary car after I left The Farmer's Arms,' she informed him rebelliously, hoping to let him know that if there was the remotest chance of her getting a lift in preference to using a bed in his room she would take it.

His expression softened suddenly. 'Trust me, Emmie,' he urged mildly. 'I know you've never shared a room with a man before, but—'

'You've soon changed your tune!' she erupted, interrupting him again. 'This morning you were of the opinion I was late because I was having too much fun in bed with some—'

'I didn't know for certain this morning—' he interrupted her this time '—that you were a virgin.'

That stopped Emmie dead in her tracks. Her cheeks went a bit pink, and she looked quickly away from him. She guessed he'd probably arrived at his correct assumption from the little he already knew of her, added to it her modesty when he tried to peel her out of her clothes.

'What—um—what about Roberta—Mrs Short?' Emmie quickly bolted up another avenue, away from her embarrassment at discussing such intimate matters.

'Naturally, as Roberta and Neville's guest myself, I've told her what I intend.'

'She—didn't object?'

He gave her a hard look, but if he was remembering that she knew he was having an affair with his hostess he gave no sign of it, but stated, 'Roberta was all for it. She's had a hot-water bottle put into your bed, and some nightwear slipped under your pillow.'

Roberta was all for it! Roberta—his mistress! Roberta,

his mistress, was all for him sharing his room with another woman! Emmie stared at him, stunned. But then she recalled how elegant Roberta had looked when she'd opened the door to her—and how bedraggled and unkempt *she* had looked, like something even the cat would have disdained to drag in—so much so Roberta hadn't recognised her. Emmie coloured again. Roberta would burst out laughing if anyone suggested Emmie was any competition!

Emmie pushed her second wave of embarrassment away, and looked at Barden Cunningham. From his tough appearance, she guessed he was expecting further argument. She recalled how—and it still stung—he had called her a prissy little Miss Prim and Proper—and suddenly, on top of her recent nightmare drive, she felt goaded beyond measure. She'd just about had enough.

She placed her empty soup mug down on the tray with a small bang, and stood up. Barden Cunningham stood up too. 'You lay just one finger on me and I'll kill you,' she hissed.

'In the unlikely event that I should ever feel that tempted,' he grunted, 'I'll kill myself!'

She hated him as they left the library, hated him as he escorted her up the long, winding staircase, and hated him with renewed ferocity when along the landing he opened a bedroom door and ushered her inside. A bedside lamp between the two beds had been switched on. Emmie was just about to antagonistically ask him which bed was his, when he left her to go into the adjoining bathroom. She heard bath water running, then he came back to her.

'Take a hot bath and get into bed,' he instructed.

But she'd had just about enough of him—and that went double for his orders. 'If it's all the same to you, I won't bother.'

He, it seemed, had equally had enough of her. 'Either I have your word that you'll have a hot bath, or I'll stay and dunk you in it myself.'

'You and whose army?'

He gave her a hard look, then without more ado took off his jacket. 'I refuse to have your pneumonia on my conscience!' he snarled, his hands at his cufflinks.

'It's news to me that you've got one!' She attempted to defy him, though backed away a step. 'Anyway…' She started to weaken when, cufflinks undone, he began to roll up his sleeves. 'It's a scientific fact that you can't catch cold from getting wet and frozen. You have to catch a virus before—' She broke off when, both sleeves rolled up, he went grimly back to the bathroom, presumably to test the temperature of the bath water. Emmie followed him. 'Oh, go back to your party!' she flung at him irritatedly.

Barden came over to her. 'Do I have your word?'

'You know you do.' She was forced to admit defeat. She led the way from the bathroom and watched as he turned his sleeves back down and did up his gold cufflinks. 'Would you really have? Dunked me in the bath, I mean?'

He smiled. 'You certainly know how to spoil a man's pleasure,' he replied, and, picking up his dinner jacket, he left her.

Spoil a man's pleasure? By giving her word and depriving him of the chance to dunk her in the bath? Oh, he'd have loved it, wouldn't he? Knowing him, he'd have had it in mind to push her head under, and hold it there for a good few seconds.

Roberta had been exceptionally kind, Emmie discovered, for alongside the masculine impedimenta in the bathroom was a fresh tablet of expensively scented soap, a new plastic-encased toothbrush and toothpaste. Perhaps out of kindness too, because of the wreck Emmie had looked, Roberta had loaned her a totally feminine concoction of a nightdress. It was of some diaphanous material that left little to the imagination. It crossed Emmie's mind to push the nightdress under Cunningham's pillow and snaffle his pyjamas.

She decided, however, that he was probably the type who went to bed *au naturel*, so didn't bother looking.

She had to admit she felt much more like her old self after taking a hot bath. So much so she even found enough energy to rinse through her smalls and place them on the hot rail to dry beneath her towel.

Her bed was bliss, the hot-water bottle a delight. Emmie was by then coming to terms with the fact that there had been absolutely no other option—she had to share a room with that womanising, two-timing swine. Womanising, but not with her, apparently—he'd die first. Well, that suited her perfectly, she fumed indignantly—though she had no idea why she should feel so indignant.

Oddly, although she felt too tired to keep her eyes open, sleep eluded her to start with. Emmie guessed it was the strangeness of having to occupy a bed in her employer's room that was making her fidget. But, thinking about it, with so many people staying over for breakfast, the party going on downstairs was probably the sort that would go on all night. By that reckoning, when Cunningham came upstairs to go to bed, she could get up and go down the stairs. Sleep arrived then. Gorgeous, much needed, energy-giving sleep.

Energy that Emmie very much required when, some time after two on Saturday morning, she was awakened by a horrendous feeling of nausea. The room was in darkness. She lay there, feeling ill and trying to adjust to where she was, what she was doing there and—oh, help, where was the bathroom!

She felt a violent surge in her stomach, and there was no time for her to wonder where the bathroom lay—seconds only to charge from her bed and hope she made it. More by luck than anything else, she instinctively bolted in the right direction; her hand found the bathroom light switch and she was just in time.

Emmie was unaware of anything as she bent over, other

than how awful she felt. So awful in fact did she feel that, instead of being alarmed when a pair of bare legs came and joined her in the bathroom, and she glanced up and saw Barden Cunningham, still tying his robe, she was more grateful than anything to see him.

'Oh, Emmie, Emmie,' he murmured, his grey eyes on her ashen complexion. Hurriedly she turned from him, feeling too ill to be embarrassed at the scantiness of her attire. A masculine hand came to hold her head—he would never know how comforting his action was.

'I'm—s-sorry,' she offered shakily, miserably, when it was over and he'd sat her on a bathroom stool.

'You've caught a chill,' he stated, for once his tone not accusing, but sensitive to how dreadful she looked and was feeling.

Emmie shook her head. 'Prawns,' she corrected. 'It has to be the prawns.'

'You had prawns?'

'A risotto—on my way here. One of them must have been off.'

'One?'

'It only takes one. Oh—excuse me!' she exclaimed urgently—and was off again. In fact, for the next three hours she was violently ill.

Twice during that time she had returned to her bed. And twice Barden, having opted to rest on his bed with the lamp between them aglow, was right there with her when she dived for the bathroom. Emmie was just beginning to wonder if it was ever going to end, when it did. Barden, too, seemed to recognise that it was finally all over as he once again helped her to sit on the bathroom stool.

She felt beaten, utterly exhausted, and was entirely without protest when he told her to look up at him. Obediently, she looked up. 'Poor little Emily,' he crooned, and gently sponged her face. 'How do you feel now?'

'Fine,' she said bravely. And went to stand up—only her legs felt weak.

Barden's arm came swiftly about her. 'Lean on me,' he suggested, and she was glad to. Slowly he took her back to her bed and sat her down. She felt his hand brush her hair back from her forehead, and knew that she was feeling better when she began to realise what a sight she must look.

'I'm a mess!' she exclaimed before she could stop herself.

Barden looked down at her, paused, and then said quietly, 'You're quite beautiful.'

That startled her. So much so she felt her heartbeat drumming. 'You're drunk,' she accused, and loved his laugh.

'You're obviously on the mend.' He smiled, and instructed her. 'Sit tight.' And while Emmie was thinking of lying down and sleeping until Christmas, he moved away and came back holding a fresh shirt. 'Your night gear's soaked,' he offered conversationally, and, vaguely aware that she had been perspiring freely while in the throes of food poisoning, Emmie, more aware of everything now than she had been, looked down to see that her nightdress was doing a very poor job of covering her.

'Oh!' she wailed. The thin straps were somewhere down her arms. Her bosom, while not over-large, was not at all small either, and her cleavage and the firm swell of her breasts were fully on display, their pink tips barely veiled by the thin damp material. With rapid haste she folded her arms in front of her.

But, while she was dying a thousand deaths, Barden took everything in his stride. 'Come on, Miss Modesty. Take that damp thing off and get into this. Okay, okay,' he said, and when she didn't move he did.

He turned his back on her and Emmie, having to stand up to do so, struggled out of her clammy nightdress and into the shirt. She hadn't buttoned it up when he turned round, so he matter-of-factly helped her. Then he was standing back, his eyes travelling over her and the long length of her legs.

'You look better in that than I do,' he commented, and, before she could think of anything to say, 'Are you going to behave yourself if I tuck you up in bed?'

She knew quite well that he was teasingly referring to her recent habit of leaving her bed to dash to the bathroom. 'Just let me sleep!' she begged, and did, more or less as soon as her head hit her pillow. She slept soundly.

Emmie surfaced around ten o'clock. She opened her eyes and, as everything came flooding back, swiftly turned, feeling utter relief—the other bed was empty. Somehow she wasn't ready to see Barden Cunningham just yet.

She checked her watch, and swung her feet over the side of the bed. Catching sight of the shirt she had on, she groaned. Oh, hang it—during the night, even though her employer had helped to button her up in his shirt, it hadn't bothered her! This morning she wanted to run away and hide.

She raised her eyes, and noticed for the first time that her suit and shirt, last seen on the library carpet, had been carefully dried and pressed and was hanging up on the outside of the wardrobe. Her never-to-be-the-same-again shoes had been dried too, and polished, and were by the dressing table. And there, on the dressing table itself, lay a fresh pack of tights.

Realising that the housekeeper must have organised everything for her, though only on Roberta Short's instructions, Emmie felt most grateful to the two of them. The more she learned about Roberta, the more she liked her—though how she and Cunningham could carry on so behind Neville Short's back was...

Emmie didn't care to think of Barden Cunningham's part in the affair, and abruptly left her bed. She discovered she was feeling a mite fragile, but told herself she was feeling fine, and, having more important things to do that day than stand around, she went to take a hasty shower. Somehow she had to get her car back on the road. She was picking up Aunt Hannah at three. Subject to road conditions, it might take Emmie all of that time to get to her.

She was dressed and was just slipping on her shoes when, opening the door very quietly, as if not to disturb her should she still be in a recovering sleep, Barden Cunningham came in. He seemed surprised to see her out of bed, and fully dressed into the bargain. But he saved his comments to ask, 'How are you feeling?'

'Fine,' she told him brightly—and found herself on the receiving end of a stern look.

'I asked how do you feel?' he repeated—a man who rarely went in for repeating himself.

He was starting to niggle her—and he'd been so good. 'How do I look?' she asked, ashamed that she could be so ungrateful, but pinning a smile on her face.

Barden studied her, and, too late remembering that she hadn't got a scrap of make-up on, that she was pale and had shadows under her eyes, Emmie sorely wished she hadn't invited his inspection.

'Delicate,' he pronounced when he'd finished his scrutiny.

Emmie pulled herself together. 'Like an orchid?' she queried with a grin, certain that she wasn't in the least bothered how he saw her.

His mouth twitched. 'You're lippy again—you're better,' he pronounced. 'Feel like some breakfast?'

That took the smile off her face. *'Don't!'* she implored, the mere thought of food making her stomach turn. She took a step away, then turned back. 'Thank you for staying with me and putting up with me—and for looking after me. You could easily have pulled your duvet over your head and let me get on with it.'

'What, and leave a maiden in distress?' he teased, and she found she liked it.

'Well, thank you anyway, Mr Cunningham,' she said sincerely—and saw his mouth twitch again. 'What...?' she began.

'We sleep together—and I'm still Mr Cunningham?' His grey eyes had the light of devilment in them.

'Not in that context!' she protested. 'We shared a room, that's—' She broke off—it had to be said that he'd seen more of her, in the literal sense, than any man she was on first-name terms with.

'I really think, Emily—' he took over when she seemed to be floundering '—that we know each other well enough for you to use my first name.'

'Yes, well...' Where had this absurd habit of suddenly blushing come from? She glanced from him, and caught sight of her shoulder bag. She couldn't remember the last time she'd had it, but, hoping she had automatically dropped her car keys inside, she went to retrieve it. 'I'd better go and rescue my car,' she announced.

'Your car's going nowhere until there's a thaw,' Barden informed her. And, before she could begin to argue, he continued, 'I've been to take a look.'

That didn't stop her. 'I thought I might get a tractor to pull me out.'

'Apparently your car wasn't the only one that went off the road last night. The non-urgent cases are being left till last. If there's no thaw before, yours will be pulled out around Monday.'

She stared at him. 'But mine *is* urgent. I have to get home. I...'

'I'll take you home.'

How could he be so matter-of-fact? 'But you're at a weekend party!' she protested. And, starting to feel all hot and bothered suddenly, she went on, 'I've already ruined last night's party for you, and...'

'Did I say you had?'

'No, but...'

'Look here, Emily Lawson, I'm driving you home today and that's it. You'll need all your concentration out there— and, frankly, you don't look up to it!'

Thanks! How did he expect her to look when she'd spent half the night being sick? Bossy swine! It hadn't taken him long to get into 'You'll do as I say' mode, had it? She'd walk first. Though, confound it, there was Aunt Hannah to think of. If she went with Cunningham now, she'd be able to take a taxi to pick her up from Keswick House. 'It's not fair to your hosts,' was the best defence she could come up with. 'You'll be gone hours, and—'

'The household's asleep, and unlikely to stir before noon,' he butted in.

Emmie realised then that all she was doing was delaying his return to his party weekend. She caved in. 'What are the roads like?'

'All main roads are clear, apparently, though getting to one is best done in daylight.'

Emmie picked up her bag. 'Is now a good time?' His answer was to escort her from the room. 'Would you thank Mr and Mrs Short for me, and their housekeeper?' she asked, as downstairs Barden undid the front door.

'Of course,' he promised, and, guiding her out to his car, kept a firm grip on her arm as they crunched over the snow.

Emmie closed her eyes from the glare of the snow—and was astonished when she opened them to find that they were leaving the main road and were heading for the area where she lived.

'I've been asleep!' she exclaimed unnecessarily. 'I'm sorry,' she quickly apologised.

'It will do you good,' Barden answered easily. 'I've an idea I must turn somewhere around here.'

Emmie came fully awake to give him directions to where she had her flat, and a short while afterwards he was steering his smart car into the run-down area where she lived, and pulling up in front of the dilapidated house where she had her flat.

'Would you like to come in for a cup of coffee before your journey back?' she asked politely, knowing in all fairness that she couldn't do anything else, but for some unknown reason, when he'd been so good, hoping he would say he had to dash back.

'Thanks,' he accepted, to her surprise, and went to the front door with her, and as she got out her keys he took them from her. Without commenting that the splintered door looked as though one slight shoulder-charge would have it open without the need for a key, he opened it and waited for her to go through.

He still had her keys when they crossed the floor to her apartment. 'This is it,' she said, and he opened the door. 'Come in,' she invited, and took him into her sitting room. The elegant contrast to the scruffy outside of the building was so marked Emmie wasn't surprised to see his glance flick over the expensive carpeting that had come first from the house where she had been born, and had then been taken to the apartment where she had lived with Alec and his mother.

'Have you lived alone long?' he enquired, his eyes skimming the good quality furniture before coming to rest on her liquid brown eyes.

That word 'commitment' reared its ugly head again. He mustn't know about Aunt Hannah! 'Not so long,' she replied. 'I'll—er—get that coffee.'

She went to move away, but Barden caught hold of her arm and detained her. 'What did I say?'

'Say?'

'You're touchy about something.'

'Pfff. You lost sleep too,' she pointed out loftily. Hoping he would read from that she thought his brain was suffering from his disturbed night, she jerked her arm out of his hold and went to her kitchen.

Had she thought, however, that by walking away from him she had put an end to the conversation, she found she was wrong. She hadn't even filled the kettle or set it to boil when Barden appeared behind her. Feeling on edge, her not-liking-him-very-much vibes on the loose again, she set about making him some coffee.

'Sugar?' she enquired, knowing full well that he didn't take it, but feeling the silence between them stretching. She didn't want him speculating on anything about her, thank you very much, but knew from the way he performed his business dealings that what he didn't know he made jolly sure he found out.

He didn't deign to reply to her sugar question, but asked instead—his tone mild, gentle even, it had to be said— 'When did your parents die, Emmie?'

She wasn't sure she was on any safer ground here, and, perversely, didn't want him using the more friendly version of her name just now. It was weakening somehow. But she could see no harm in telling him what he wanted to know. 'My father died when I was ten; my mother five years later.'

'You can't have lived alone since you were fifteen?'

Emmie stared at him, startled. Honestly! 'Is it *that* important?' she asked crossly.

He smiled. She hated him. 'Remember what I said about humouring me?' She'd like to take a hatchet and humour him by burying it in his skull!

'I had a stepfather!' she stated hostilely.

'You didn't get on?'

'We did,' she contradicted. 'I loved him. He…' her anger faded. 'He died about a year ago.' She glanced up at Barden, knowing she wasn't going to tell him another word about her family—her job was too precious to now tell him she had been sparing with the truth at her job interview.

His expression had taken on a gentle look. 'You've been

through a bad time. Have you any other family?' he asked softly.

Oh, crumbs! She turned her back on him. The answer had to be a straight yes or no. Did step-grandmothers count? Suddenly she realised she was hesitating too long. 'No!' she said quickly. And, turning to take a quick glance at him, didn't miss the shrewd look in his eyes. 'I'm sorry,' she apologised once more, and, hastily striving to excuse her delay in answering—he was sharp, too sharp; she didn't want him poking his nose in where it didn't belong; he'd ferreted enough into her background in her opinion—she said firmly, 'I think last night's performance must have taken more out of me than I realised. I've—er—come over very tired.'

Barden Cunningham stared down into her pale face. 'You're all eyes!' he murmured after a moment, and then, as decisive as ever, he announced, 'Forget the coffee—I'll get off. You, Emily Lawson, take yourself off to bed.' Having issued his orders, he unexpectedly took a hold of both her arms and, while she stared up at him, mesmerised, he bent down and laid a chaste kiss on her forehead.

Her heartbeat seemed to go into overdrive, and hastily she pushed him away. 'I haven't b-been *that* ill!' she exclaimed, feeling shaken as much by the agitated drumming of her heart as his action.

His answer was to give a smile that charmed her to the core. Without another word he went on his way. Emmie collapsed onto a chair. My stars—no wonder women fell for him like ninepins. Not that she would, of course, womanising swine!

CHAPTER FOUR

THERE was no time for Emmie to go to bed as ordered. In any case she was feeling better by the minute. She made sure everything was ready for Aunt Hannah, and decided to go and collect the old lady straight away. The major roads were clear, but the lesser ones still might not be, and in consequence she might not be the only one availing herself of a taxi service.

'Where's your car?' Aunt Hannah wanted to know.

'I ran off the road in last night's snow,' Emmie replied, and, having assured the dear love that she was fine and that nothing was broken, sat in the back of the taxi with her step-relative, who seemed to have motorcycles on the brain at the moment. Aunt Hannah regaled her with a tale of how once, she on her Norton and Piggy Etheridge on his Panther, they had both skidded on ice and ended up in a snowdrift.

Save for having some misguided notion that they would be paying a visit to the National Motorcycle Museum that very day, Aunt Hannah was quite alert, Emmie felt. True Aunt Hannah decided around six o'clock, despite the fact that it was dark, that she'd like to go for a walk...

'The pavements may be icy.' Emmie attempted to put Aunt Hannah off.

'We'll walk in the road.'

They took a stroll around the block, with Aunt Hannah in excellent spirits when Emmie suggested, weather permitting, that they could go to the Motorcycle Museum next Saturday. Feeling better for their walk, Emmie helped her step-grandmother out of the layers of outer clothing she'd insisted she wear and set about preparing an early dinner.

70

They were in the kitchen washing up afterwards when the phone rang. Emmie went to answer it. 'Hello?' she said—and experienced a sudden surge of adrenalin when she recognised Barden Cunningham's voice!

'I rang earlier. You must have been out,' he commented.

'Oh, yes. Yes, I was,' she replied, but hurriedly got herself together. 'Is there something wrong with the minutes?' she enquired. He was bothering with minutes? On a Saturday night? When he was partying!

'I wondered how you were? If your system was fully clear of its bug?'

'Oh, isn't that kind!' she exclaimed softly.

And heard a smile in his voice as he teased, 'I was concerned you might be doing an action replay—with no one there to hold your head.'

Emmie laughed, and felt so at ease with him suddenly that she was totally off her guard when she responded brightly, 'Oh, I'm not on my own. I—' She broke off. Oh Lord, he mustn't know about Aunt Hannah.

'You have company?' he questioned sharply. My word—what had happened to his teasing?

It was too late now to deny it. Emmie got herself together—her 'company' could be just about anybody, for goodness' sake! He wasn't to know *who!* 'Yes,' she replied. 'Yes, I have.' Had she anything to add to that, Emmie found she would have been talking to herself—the line went dead.

She went slowly back to the kitchen, pondering on the abrupt termination of the phone call. *Now* what had she done? For certain she had upset him in some way. In no time he'd gone from pleasant and teasing to terse and snarly. Perhaps, knowing now that she had someone with her, he was regretting that, out of concern for his employee, he had taken time away from his partying to check on her.

In compensation for not cooking a meal for Adrian Payne on Friday, Emmie popped up to his flat and invited him to

Sunday lunch. Aunt Hannah insisted on calling Adrian David a few times, but the lunch passed pleasantly enough. Adrian offered to drive Emmie to look at her car the evening of the following day, hopefully to retrieve it.

Adrian was a mature college student, and left them about four to finish a paper required for the next morning. 'David seems quite a nice boy,' Aunt Hannah muttered when he'd gone.

Adrian was twenty-six if he was a day. 'He is nice,' Emmie replied, aware that Aunt Hannah hadn't really taken to Adrian but was doing her charitable best.

Aunt Hannah decided at half past four that she wanted to go back to Keswick House. Emmie went with her in a taxi, and returned to her flat to check her wardrobe for the morning.

By Monday Emmie was almost fully recovered from her food poisoning, though she awakened with a splitting headache. She downed a couple of aspirin, sneezed, but refused to contemplate any notion that she might have a cold coming on.

Because she was going to have to use public transport, she left home much earlier than usual, and gave herself a pat on the back because she arrived at her office at ten to nine.

Both Barden Cunningham and Dawn Obrey were in the office Emmie shared with Dawn when she went in. Feeling cheerful—there might have been a blip on her attendance record on Friday morning, but her time-keeping, under difficult circumstances, was perfect today— She greeted them both cheerfully, 'Good morning!'

'Good morning.' Dawn smiled. Barden scowled.

Was it *her* fault he'd got a hangover? She'd found her aspirins, but Emmie hoped he never found his. Serve him right, partying the weekend away *and* abusing the hospitality of his lover's husband! How could he?

Emmie, her feelings of cheerfulness thoroughly dampened by thoughts of the affair Cunningham was having with his friend's wife, got on with some work. The only bright spot of that day was that a thaw had set in. Adrian was meeting her from work, and, all being well, she would be able to have her car back tonight.

Plans for collecting her car went from her mind, however, as she became more and more involved in her work. In fact she had forgotten most everything but the intricate job in hand when, just as Barden Cunningham's door opened and he came in to have a word with Dawn, the phone went. He'd had a wasted journey—Dawn was out of the office, so, sucks boo. Emmie answered the phone. The call was from Keswick House.

'Mrs Whitford's let herself out of the building again, without telling anyone where she's going,' Lisa Browne told her worriedly.

Emmie, aware that Barden was looking enquiringly, as if wanting to know whether the call was for him, looked down at her desk as she strove to stay calm. 'How long ago?'

'I've checked round. About an hour or more. Apparently her absence was noticed half an hour ago, but since it only takes five minutes to get to the local shops it was thought Mrs Whitford would soon be back. She's usually back, though, long before this.'

'Has...?' Emmie began, but Lisa Browne had read her thoughts.

'I sent someone to look locally for her—they've just come back now. They've scoured round—there's no sign. Do you think she's gone back to your old home?'

Emmie's concerns by then were centred solely on Aunt Hannah. She wasn't even aware that her employer, her busy employer, was in the same room with her when she answered, 'I think there's every chance. Leave it with me; I'll go and look.'

She replaced the phone, glanced up—and stark reality

hit. Cool grey eyes were studying her, watching, waiting. Oh, heavens, she was going to have to ask him for time off. Oh, crumbs, she needed this job! Only just then her need to find Aunt Hannah had priority.

Emmie was already reaching for her bag, while holding down her anxiety, as she told Barden, 'I'm sorry, I need an hour or so off.'

His look was cool. 'Man-friend trouble?' he rapped, and Emmie stared at him. Why would he think that? Probably because he was under the impression she had no family—and the fact she'd been 'entertaining' when he'd rung on Saturday evening, she realised.

But she hadn't time to bother with such things then. 'I—have to dash!' she stated stubbornly, on her feet and hoping with all she had that an hour off was all she would need.

'Your—errand seems urgent?' he questioned. Emmie refused to answer; she was worried—he was unsympathetic. 'You haven't a car!' he reminded her, clearly not liking her mulish silence.

'I'll get a taxi.'

'*That* urgent!'

Emmie nodded dumbly, feeling that her job was on the line here, but knowing she'd lose it for sure if he found out she had lied at her job interview. She knew, however, from the sudden look of purpose about him that he'd come to a decision—she prayed it wasn't one of the Don't-bother-to-come-back variety.

Emmie had her prayer answered, though nearly dropped with shock when, revealing his decision, Barden said crisply, 'No need for a taxi. I'll take you.'

'*No!*' rocketed from her in panic, before she could hold it back.

He smiled, an insincere smile. 'Get your coat,' he ordered. The door opened and Dawn came in, 'I have to go out for about an hour, Dawn. I'll take Emily with me. Contact me on my mobile if you need me.'

Emmie hated Barden-bossy-Cunningham as they crossed the car park. She loathed and detested him as she climbed into the passenger seat of his car. But, over and above all that, she was extremely anxious and stewed up about her missing step-relative.

The engine was running. 'Your flat?' Barden enquired pleasantly.

She didn't trust that pleasant tone—why couldn't he keep his nose out of her business? Emmie knew quite well that she should be grateful that he had volunteered to drive her, but she didn't feel at all so. The only reason he'd volunteered was because he had an over-large curiosity gene. All she'd done by refusing to explain why she wanted an hour off was to stir his proclivity to find out what he didn't know.

'No,' she replied frostily, and perforce was obliged to give him directions to her previous apartment—and found something more to worry about.

It was only last Friday that Aunt Hannah had once more taken off. While Emmie's main concern now was to get to her and find her safe, she couldn't help but wonder how Lisa Browne would view it if it happened much more. She wouldn't want to send her care assistants out looking every time the dear love decided that rules were only there to be broken. But Aunt Hannah was happy at Keswick House— what if they asked her to leave?

Realising she had enough to worry about for now, without looking for future problems, Emmie saw that they were driving through a very salubrious area and were almost at their destination. 'If you'll slow down here,' she found her voice to request, 'and take a right here.' Another left turn and they were at the terrace of elegant houses. 'If you'd let me out here,' she said quietly. There was no sign of Aunt Hannah anywhere, but she'd just get rid of Cunningham first—if she couldn't find her aunt in the area she'd taxi back to her current flat. 'Thank you for the lift. I'll get back to the office as soon as I can,' she added prettily—fingers crossed she'd still got a job. With that, and without turning to look at him, Emmie got out of the car and walked to the main door of her old home.

All the while, though, she was conscious that her employer had not driven by her. What was he playing at? She concentrated on more pressing matters and went up the steps to the front door.

Before she could ring the bell, however, the door opened and Johnnie Jeavons, a man of thirty-two years and one of the nicest people she knew, came out. 'Emmie!' he exclaimed, and, delighted to see her, he leaned over and kissed her cheek. 'Come in,' he invited. 'Jane's home; we're both having a day off work.'

Emmie quickly explained that she was only in the area because Mrs Whitford, who was perfectly fine, sometimes absently arrived at the wrong address.

'She always was a card!' Johnnie recollected. 'Do you remember that time she told the postman to change his route and send another one, because he never brought her any news but bad?'

Emmie did, but, much as she liked Johnnie, she was more concerned with finding Aunt Hannah. Emmie found a piece of paper in her bag and wrote down her home and office phone numbers. 'Would you mind giving me a ring if Mrs Whitford comes by?' she asked, handing the paper over, knowing for sure that Johnnie would invite Aunt Hannah in and give her a cup of tea while he rang her.

'With pleasure,' he smiled. 'I'll just slip up now and give this to Jane.'

Emmie thanked him, took a step to leave, and again thought what a nice person Johnnie was when he kissed her cheek again before letting her go. Her mind was back on Aunt Hannah before she reached the bottom of the steps. Emmie looked about and, not a sign of her aunt, caught sight instead of the long sleek car she had arrived in! Oh grief, she'd forgotten *him*!

That Barden Cunningham was still there, had sat there watching while she'd greeted Johnnie Jeavons, was no figment of her imagination. Why had he stayed? From the cold look on his face, the waiting had not given him any pleasure.

Ideally she would have liked to have walked on by him. Only the thought of how humiliating it would be if he took it into his head to follow her, with his car purring at a crawl, stopped her. She went up to the driver's window. The window slid down.

She opened her mouth to again appeasingly thank him, and hint he should be on his way, but he got in first. 'That it?' he clipped, which wrong-footed her.

'That what?'

He tossed her an exasperated look. 'Get in!' he rapped.

'I…' She looked away, her glance lighting on Johnnie, who smiled and waved. She found a smile and waved back. Humiliating! She went round to the passenger door and got in. Barden started up the car and moved off. By the time he had driven around the corner, however, Emmie had got herself into more of one piece. 'I—er—haven't finished my—business yet,' she informed him as evenly as she was able.

'That *wasn't* it?'

She had felt like hitting him before, but hadn't. Now she sorely felt like making up for lost time. 'I'll get a taxi!' she retorted.

He ignored her. 'Where to now?' he gritted.

She took a deep and steadying breath. She had an idea she was close to losing her job anyway—so what the heck? 'If you could just drive around the area for a few minutes.'

To his credit, he didn't demand to know why. 'Intriguing!' he commented.

'Look, you needn't…I can…'

'Wouldn't dream of letting you,' he came back with phoney charm, adding pithily, 'I can't think of anything I'd rather be doing!'

What could she say? Nothing. If she didn't so badly need to hang on to her job, and the good salary it paid, she might have told him to get lost anyway. But she did need to hang on. Quite desperately did she need to. So she stayed silent, and as he steered his car around the block, and while her eyes scanned frantically for the person she was looking for, Emmie at the same time tried to behave as if she was perfectly relaxed.

They returned to the point from where they had started. 'Again?' he enquired sardonically. She was going to hit him soon!

Her searching eyes could see no sign of Aunt Hannah. 'Would you drive to my home, please?' she requested, knowing by then she'd be wasting her breath if she again suggested that he let her out so she might take a taxi. 'Would you drive slowly, please?'

He turned and cast a glance at her. 'Suddenly you're carsick?'

She ignored him, sarcastic swine! She'd travelled miles with him before with no ill effect, and he knew it. And, if anything, she felt flushed rather than pale, so knew she wasn't looking as if the car's motion was making her feel queasy.

For all Barden had slowed his speed, it didn't take them all that long to approach the decrepit area where Emmie now lived. She was still scanning everywhere when, suddenly, her searching eyes were rewarded. *'Stop!'* she ordered on catching sight of Aunt Hannah, standing admiring a parked enormous motorcycle.

'What the...?' Barden's reactions were instant.

'I'm sorry.' Awash with relief, Emmie was ready to apologise ten times over, and more quietly requested, 'Would you pull over please, Barden?' Where had his first name come from?

Feeling slightly shattered, and wondering if the worry of her missing step-relative had weakened her brain, Emmie waited only until he'd found a convenient place to park, and then she was out of the car.

Emmie hurried the first few yards, but then, not wanting to startle Aunt Hannah by pouncing on her, she slowed her pace.

'Hello, Aunt Hannah,' she greeted her quietly as she reached her.

Mrs Whitford dragged her gaze from the motorcycle. 'Hello, dear,' she answered, seeming not the least surprised to see her there when she should be at work. 'What do you think of that? It's a Harley,' she explained. 'A Harley-Davidson. Isn't it beautiful!'

'Quite beautiful,' Emmie agreed; to her non-mechanical mind, one piece of machinery was very like another.

She was just about to tactfully suggest Aunt Hannah came with her—for all there was a thaw it was still wintry, and the elderly lady shouldn't be standing about on a day like today—when Emmie realised they had company. Tall, good-looking, not saying a word, her employer had come to join them. The word 'commitment' jetted into her head, and as anxiety rushed in again her feelings of relief were short-lived. Why couldn't Barden Cunningham have stayed in his car? Another few minutes and she might have thought of something. As it was, with him so close, her thinking power seemed to have seized up.

But she had been very well brought up. 'Aunt Hannah.' She drew the dear love's attention away from the motor-bike. 'This is Barden Cunningham. Er, B-Barden...' She couldn't look at him, and, as more and more of her hopes of keeping her job went trickling down the drain, she said, 'this is my step-grandmother, Mrs Whitford.'

He appeared not a whit put out. Emmie guessed he never

would be. If her manners were good, his were impeccable as he extended his right hand to Aunt Hannah and shook hands with her, and enquired politely, 'May I give you a lift somewhere? My car is just here.'

'Are you Emmie's friend?' Aunt Hannah wanted to know.

'We see a lot of each other,' he fielded smoothly.

Mrs Whitford stared sternly at him. 'You're not her lover?' she questioned—making Emmie's ears go pink.

'Aunt Hannah,' she rushed in before he could answer, 'you'll get cold standing about in...'

'I won't,' she answered with a saintly smile. 'I remember what you said on Saturday about wrapping up warmly before we went out. I've got dozens of layers on.'

'You kept Emmie company on Saturday evening?' Barden asked, and Emmie felt her pugilistic tendencies rearing again. What he didn't know, he found out! Though why he should want to bother finding out if her step-relative was the person she had been with when he rang on Saturday stumped her.

But in any event Aunt Hannah wasn't in an answering frame of mind. 'Have you got the time?' she asked him, 'I believe I'm hungry.' And, not waiting to be told the time, she stated, 'I think I'll go back.'

'I'll take you, sweetheart,' Emmie said gently, fully aware that if Aunt Hannah had been wandering around for the last couple of hours she must be extremely tired.

Emmie was again thinking in terms of hailing a taxi when Barden took a hold of Mrs Whitford's arm. 'My car's the black one, just here,' he said, taking charge. 'Where do you live?' he asked conversationally.

'Keswick,' she answered brightly, and Emmie felt an insane desire to laugh. Keswick was a town miles away, in the Lake District—Barden, who'd got a full afternoon scheduled, as she well knew, would never make it to Keswick and back before dark!

As he began to steer Mrs Whitford to his car he glanced across at Emmie, as if seeking confirmation that her step-relative's destination truly was in the north of England, and Emmie had to quickly banish her serves-you-right look. Well—it was he who'd insisted she shouldn't take a taxi. He who had insisted he drove her around London. He who wouldn't take no for an answer. But—this wasn't funny! There were going to be repercussions—Emmie just knew it.

'It's about five miles away,' she informed him quietly, but was not thanked for the information. After he unlocked his car, either from courtesy to Aunt Hannah or because he'd had quite enough of one Emily Lawson, he assisted her step-relative into the front passenger seat.

I know my place, Emmie mused whimsically, and got into the rear of the car to discover that, while sometimes the needle on Aunt Hannah's memory groove occasionally slipped, she had no such problem in giving him directions to where she lived.

'Do you have a motorcycle?' she asked him chattily— and, not a word coming Emmie's way, the two in front carried on a pleasant conversation with regard to Aunt Hannah's long-term love affair with motorcycles.

They arrived at Keswick House, and Barden Cunningham again took charge. It was his arm Mrs Whitford leant on as he escorted her from his car to the front door. He to whom she turned and suggested he drop in for a cup of tea whenever he was passing.

But, to prove that her memory did occasionally get a little fogged—unless she was being deliberately forgetful, which wouldn't have surprised Emmie in this instance— she turned to her as they entered the building, and said affectionately, 'You're a good girl. Too good for that David.' Leaving Emmie undecided if she was being wicked or not. 'Are you going to marry him?'

Wicked, Emmie decided. 'I'll let you know when he asks me,' she smiled.

'Bye, darling. See you Saturday.'

'Shall I come to your room with you?' Emmie offered, wanting to help her aunt out of her coat, hat and scarf, but appreciating her independent spirit.

'No, thank you, dear. I want to go and have a word with Mrs Vellacott first.' She turned to Barden, 'Thank you for the lift,' she said graciously.

Vicky, one of the care assistants, came hurrying forward just then. 'Mrs Whitford!' she exclaimed in a relieved kind of voice. 'We've been so worried about you.'

'Absolutely no need, Victoria!' Aunt Hannah replied firmly. And, her voice carrying back loud and clear as she went off in search of her friend, to Emmie's horror, she added, 'I've been out with my granddaughter and her fiancé.'

It had been in Emmie's head to go and find Lisa Browne and have a quick word. But all such thoughts went flying as she turned scarlet with mortification, unable to look at Barden Cunningham to see how he was taking the news that he—free, a womaniser, and not looking to change that state of affairs—had just acquired an appendage likely to cramp his style.

She reeled out to his car and, because he held the door open for her, got into the front passenger seat, her pleasure that that was the first time she'd heard Aunt Hannah refer to her as her granddaughter spoilt by the rest of it. 'I'm so sorry—about that.' She found a choky kind of voice when he joined her in the car—was there ever such a foul pig of a day? 'Aunt H… Mrs Whitford—' Emmie broke off. She would defend Aunt Hannah to death, but had to give him some sort of an explanation. 'Mrs Whitford sometimes gets, just a bit confused,' she resumed. 'She'll have—'

'Forget it!' he clipped.

Emmie was happy to. But she feared the worst when she

noticed that they weren't driving in a direction that would take them back to the office, but away from it! Her heart sank down into her boots when she saw that they were nearing the area where she lived. And, the closer they got to her flat, the more she realised that her suspicions were correct. He could, she supposed, have left her to make her own way back from Keswick House. Though she hardly felt like thanking him, because by dropping her off at her home he had to be letting her know that there was no place for her at the office. This was it; she was sacked, fired, dismissed.

Barden pulled up outside the decrepit building where she had her home. Perhaps she should tell him goodbye, but she just couldn't find her voice. She stepped out of the car and went to her outer door, searching in her bag for her keys.

She found them, but jerked her head up when a cool hand stretched out and took them from her. She hadn't expected him to get out of the car too, and stared at him. She realised she must be feeling quite stunned because, as daft as you like, she handed her keys over.

Emmie had managed to retrieve a few of her scattered wits by the time he had the door unlocked. She held out her hand for the return of her keys, but was startled when he held on to them and, pushing the door open, indicated she should precede him into the building.

And that was when her stubborn streak reasserted itself. She refused to move another step. Her stubborn streak was short-lived, however—he killed it. Barden stared down at her immovable expression, his own expression tough.

'You owe me a cup of coffee!' he reminded her evenly—and Emmie understood then. Her dismissal was to be a verbal one, and, his manners impeccable, as already demonstrated—if one forgot what a rat he was when it came to other men's wives—it was not his intention to give her a dressing-down in the street.

Emmie, as proud as the next, was glad about that. 'Come in,' she invited, and went first.

Barden undid the door to her apartment while Emmie strove not to think of her perilous financial position, or the fact that he was highly unlikely to give her a decent reference—and how her future work prospects for anywhere that didn't pay peanuts looked bleak.

They were in her comfortable sitting room when Emmie turned to face him. 'Would you care to sit down?' she suggested, doing her best in the circumstances to be civil, to remember her own manners.

Barden stared at her from cool grey eyes. 'After you!' he replied curtly, and she knew then, as she took the seat nearest to her, that he was no more interested in a cup of coffee than she was. Nor was he wasting any more of his precious time. Taking the seat opposite, he at once demanded, 'Was the whole of your interview a lie?'

Straight to the nitty-gritty! Typical of him, of course. 'My qualifications were—are—as stated,' she replied.

'But not your reasons for taking temporary work after Usher Trading folded?'

Emmie didn't see why she should answer; her job with him was at an end, whatever she said, so why bother? Though, on second thoughts, he *had* taken a huge chunk out of his morning to take her around looking for Aunt Hannah—even though it must have seemed something like a wild-goose chase to him. And she had never liked being dishonest with him anyway. Nor did she need to be dishonest with him, she realised. He had found out about her commitment, her lie, and she was getting what she deserved. He was straightforward in all his business dealings—he wouldn't countenance having anyone in his office who didn't likewise measure up.

'No,' she admitted at long last.

'Your employment after Usher Trading always ended in dismissal?' he queried.

How did he know that? 'It got to be a habit,' she answered flippantly. Was all this necessary? He was terminating her services, so…

'Why?' he wanted to know, ignoring her flippancy.

'Why what? Why did it become a habit?'

'I've no quarrel with your work,' he answered. 'You said you were good, and you are.'

His compliment to her work was unexpected—and weakening. 'I wasn't always dismissed,' she told him. 'Sometimes I just walked out.'

'I'm aware you've a fiery temperament.' *Her? Fiery temperament?* 'But would you like to tell me why, when I know you need work, you let your temper get the better of you?'

Cunningham was a womaniser—like she was going to tell *him*! 'No,' she replied, 'I wouldn't.'

Barden studied her speculatively for a moment or so, his glance raking her flushed features, her wooden expression. 'Then I'll tell you,' he pronounced. Go on then, clever clogs—bet you get it wrong. But, in the main, he didn't. 'You were sacked, mostly, for absenteeism and appalling time-keeping.'

'You guessed!' she fumed—the headache with which she had awakened was back again.

'I have it in writing,' he replied.

Astonished, she stared at him. 'In—writing?' she echoed faintly.

'Personnel have a policy of sending for references, whether requested by heads of departments or not.' Oh, hang it! References! She'd thought she'd got away with… 'Usually they're just kept on file. But, despite the fact I hadn't asked for them, when all your four references were to hand, Garratt in Personnel felt I should take a look at them.'

'How long…?'

'The last one arrived on Friday morning.'

'When I—didn't!' she said, and felt utterly miserable—until pride woke up and gave her a nudge. 'You're right, my time-keeping was appalling, but I always more than made up for any time I lost.'

'And your unmitigated rudeness,' he went on. 'According to Smythe and Wood International—'

'Unmitigated!' she flew. 'Mitigated, I'd say. Clive Norris was always hinting—without the smallest encouragement—that he and I could be doing better things than work. When he backed me into a corner, then made a lascivious grab for me, yes, I was rude!'

'He made advances?'

Emmie stared hostilely across at Barden. 'Not for nothing! I hit him, and walked—and kept on walking.' She thought his look had softened a little—but knew she would still be out of a job. 'And, yes, too, I'm sorry I lied to you about the reason I left my temporary jobs, but...'

'You felt you had to?' he questioned toughly, any softening she'd imagined clearly a mirage.

'I'm not usually a liar,' she stated. 'But—er—circumstances were against me.'

'Circumstances?'

He had a right to be answered, to be answered truthfully, she knew that, but his delving to the heart of the matter was starting to irritate her. She was out of a job, so you'd think he'd stop his probing!

Emmie shrugged. 'I've said I'm sorry I lied to you.' She was feeling stubborn again, and not intending to say anything more.

That was until she met his no-nonsense cool grey eyes again. 'You're sorry you lied about why you left your other *permanent* jobs?'

Swine! So, okay, she'd hoped they'd be permanent when she'd started them. Was it her fault that there were such womanising fiends about—not to mention the one in front of her? Though—her innate honesty tripped her up—in all fairness she hadn't left *every* job because of male lechery. In some cases her time-keeping *had* had something to do with it.

'I'm sorry as well,' she apologised, 'that when you asked if I had any commitments I said no. Not that I think of my step-grandmother as a commitment,' she said hurriedly. 'I just felt that in the context of your question I wouldn't have stood a chance if I'd told you the truth.'

He didn't give her any marks for perception, but questioned, 'Mrs Whitford is your *only* family?' In view of the fact she'd told him on Saturday that she didn't have any family at all, Emmie supposed she shouldn't be too surprised by the emphasis of his question.

'Yes,' she admitted quietly.

'And is Mrs Whitford the reason for your previous erratic time-keeping—the reason you didn't make it at all last Friday morning?'

Emmie nodded. 'I thought she was better. Aunt Hannah started to become a bit confused shortly after her son, my stepfather, died,' she explained. 'But she's been much more settled lately. Living at Keswick House, where she has company all day, seemed to be suiting her much better.'

'She's recently moved there?'

'Yes,' Emmie agreed. 'Aunt Hannah's supposed to write where she's going in the ''Out'' book, or at least tell someone where she's off to when she goes out, but on Friday, and again this morning, she didn't.'

'So Keswick House rang you?'

'They sent someone looking for her when they missed her. When they couldn't find her Mrs Browne rang me, wondering if Aunt Hannah had gone back to our old apartment. She—er—sometimes used to.'

'That would be the first address we went to?'

'As you saw, she wasn't there.'

'Who was the kissing doorman?' he enquired toughly, and Emmie blinked.

'Johnnie, you mean?' she asked, startled.

'We weren't introduced.'

'Johnnie's an old neighbour. I asked him to give me a ring if my step-grandmother turned up there.'

'How long ago did you leave that address?' Barden asked, and Emmie wondered what tack he was on now.

'Not so long ago,' she prevaricated, starting to feel antagonistic and deciding she'd answered enough of her ex-employer's questions.

Barden studied her for a few moments, and then caused her to realise that what he didn't know he was quite capable of correctly deducing. 'You left about the same time that Mrs Whitford moved into Keswick House,' he decided.

She decided she didn't like him. 'So?' she said mulishly.

'So you gave up your home because you could more easily afford to pay for Mrs Whitford's new accommodation if you moved somewhere less expensive.'

The sauce of it! Who did he think he was? Prodding and prying! Emmie was on her feet; she'd had enough. 'Wrong!' she corrected him coldly, and, glancing around at her mother's beautiful furniture, added, 'The walls may be different, but I still have the same home that I grew up with. And, for your information, Mrs Whitford has her own money with which to pay for her new accommodation.'

'All of it?' he enquired, on his feet too, and staring down at her. 'You don't help out at all?'

What a *pig* he was. 'I'll show you out!' was the best she could manage by way of a courteous reply. She took two paces—he didn't take one. He, it seemed, hadn't finished his inquisition yet.

'Who's David?' he wanted to know.

'David?' The question threw her, and took the edge off her anger. 'David?' she enquired again.

'The man you may marry,' he enlightened her crisply.

'Ah!' she exclaimed as light dawned. 'Adrian,' she corrected—welcome to my batty world. 'His name's Adrian, not David. Adrian's taking me to collect my car tonight.' She turned away and took another step towards showing her ex-employer out.

Only to halt in her tracks when he drawled. 'You'd better ring and cancel that arrangement.' Emmie turned. She had not the smallest intention of taking any more of his orders.

'Why would you imagine I'd do anything of the sort?' she questioned snappily.

Cool grey eyes stared down into fiery dark brown ones. 'We've a lot to do—I'm sure you won't want to keep him hanging about.'

Her heartbeat suddenly set up a hopeful commotion. She schooled herself to stay calm—this could be the biggest let-down of all time, a punishment. 'I'm—er—not quite with you?'

He smiled then, a smile she quite liked. 'I'll take you to pick up your car after we've finished.'

'Finished?' she questioned—was he saying he hadn't, after all, dismissed her?

Apparently he was. 'You're working late,' he replied succinctly, and stepped past her—leading the way out of her apartment building. Emmie, quickly overcoming her incredulity, hurried after him.

CHAPTER FIVE

EMMIE—her relief knowing no bounds that she still had a job—duly got in touch with Adrian to let him know that she wouldn't require his help that evening after all, then tried to concentrate on her work. Thoughts of Barden Cunningham, however, seemed continually to get in the way.

She quite liked him again, though she didn't want a repeat of the third degree he'd given her. A necessary third degree, she realised. He couldn't have anyone in his office who wasn't trustworthy. She rather thought that now he knew all that there was to know about her background, and why she'd found it necessary to lie to him about the commitment issue, he would also know that she *was* trustworthy. She did so hope so. Somehow, and she didn't know why, since he was being less than a trustworthy friend to Neville Short, it seemed important to her that Barden trusted her.

She continued to hold the view that if she *had* explained anything about her wandering step-grandparent at her job interview, then it would have ended right there. But by now she had apparently proved her capability—hadn't Barden agreed that her work was good?—and, miracle of miracles, *she still had her job*!

She was going to work hard and be better than good, she determined, and remembered how charming Barden had been to Aunt Hannah. She recalled the easy and well mannered way he'd behaved with her step-relative, the way he'd chatted about motorcycles with her on the way to Keswick House.

Emmie was just deciding that, yes, she really, really liked

90

Barden, when Dawn broke into her train of thought. 'It's ten past five. Unless you need help with anything, I think I'll make tracks for home.' Dawn smiled.

'You go, I'm fine here,' Emmie assured her.

'You haven't forgotten I've an appointment in the morning and won't be in until after eleven?'

Emmie hadn't forgotten, and wished Dawn well for her antenatal appointment in the morning. After Dawn had gone, she reflected that, regardless of the fact that his senior PA wouldn't be in for the first few hours tomorrow, if she, Emily Lawson, hadn't given Barden the answers he sought back at her flat—had he not assured himself of her integrity—then no way would he have told her, 'You're working late'. However, this was not the way to start being better than good.

For the next two and a half hours, Emmie put every effort into her tasks. She sneezed a couple of times, but she didn't have time to have a cold. Besides which, she was feeling on top of the world about just about everything. She no longer had to worry about keeping dear Aunt Hannah a dark and deadly secret. Hopefully, Aunt Hannah would settle down again and everything would go back to normal.

Emmie was just tidying her desk, and thinking that, with her security back, all was right, wonderfully right, with her world, when the connecting door opened and Barden came through.

'Much more to do?' he enquired pleasantly.

'Just finished,' she replied in kind, and a short while later they were travelling along the same route she had travelled on Friday night, though this time the difference in the road conditions was astonishing.

'Your car was pulled out, by the way,' Barden thought to mention as they turned off the main road.

'Did you arrange it?'

'It seemed the least I could do, considering you risked

life and limb on my behalf.' In the darkness his voice sounded as if it had a smile in it—she liked that too.

'You'd never think, tonight, that the roads were such a nightmare on Friday,' she commented.

'But the Mountie got through,' he teased, and Emmie felt her heart actually flutter with her liking for him.

They found her car parked on the side of the road. Barden went over with her to check it out. Her vehicle, illuminated by his car's headlights, seemed unscathed. He stayed with her while she got in and started up the engine.

Emmie wound down her window. 'How's that for a motor? Started first time,' she remarked happily.

Barden bent down to her, but while she thought that he had done so to listen to the engine, in order to gauge if she would make it home without problem, she found he was looking at her.

She stared at him, seemed hypnotised, couldn't look away. Nor could she move, she discovered when, his head coming nearer, he said, 'Do you know, Emily Lawson—I think—you're rather a very nice person.' Emmie was still sitting there in a kind of daze when Barden touched his wonderful mouth to hers. It was a gentle kiss, a brief kiss, and she had still not found a word of protest when, as he started to straighten up, he bade her, 'Drive carefully, Emmie.'

Emmie had been on the road a full five minutes before she came out of her shock. Not shock particularly that Barden had kissed her, brief and unexpected as it had been, but shock that when she would have objected strongly had some other employer tried it, she hadn't minded at all. In fact—she had quite liked the gentle feel of his mouth on hers!

Five minutes after that, Emmie had truly got herself back together. Stupid, stupid! The cold weather must have dramatically slowed down her reaction time. What she should have done was to have given him a mighty shove. For crying out loud—his mistress lived so close to where they'd rescued her car; the rotten hound was probably kissing her right this very minute! He might think one Emily Lawson was a rather nice person, but she wished she could say the same about him!

The fact, however, that she *could* say that about him, was brought home to her the very next morning. She awoke with a high temperature, sneezed several times and, as her head began to pound, didn't know which to reach for first—aspirin or tissues.

Feeling like death, she dragged herself to the office and was straight away called on the intercom. 'I'm not taking calls for the next hour,' Barden told her.

She swallowed so her voice should come out clear. 'Right,' she said. It was enough. Barden had nothing else to say; either he had some top executive with him, or he was working on complex matters.

During the next half-hour Emmie deflected several phone calls, then Roberta Short rang, wanting to have a word with Barden. Oh, goodness, now what did she do?

'I'm—sorry, Mrs Short, but Mr Cunningham asked not to be interrupted. May I...?'

'Not to worry.' Roberta Short was sounding joyful and disposed to have a chat. 'The house is so quiet now—the last of our *weekend* guests went on their way this morning, and this is the first chance I've had to speak to Barden. How are you, by the way? None the worse for being frozen on Friday, I hope?'

'No, I'm fine,' Emmie replied, aware that her voice was quite husky from her cold but doing her best to disguise it. 'Thank you very much for putting me up for the night,' she added courteously, suddenly most grateful to Barden, because it seemed as though he hadn't shared the cringing secret of her ghastly parting with her supper with anyone.

'It was the least we could do,' Roberta answered, apparently not a bit put out that Emmie had slept in the same room as 'her' man.

Emmie wasn't happy with such thoughts, and quickly changed the subject, hoping to end the call, by saying, 'I'm sure your party was a tremendous success. I'll—'

'With Barden organising it, it couldn't have been anything else,' Roberta cut in before Emmie could tell her that she'd let him know she had rung.

'Barden?' Emmie found she couldn't hold back from querying—when really it was absolutely none of her business. Though it was true, Roberta Short *was* being very friendly.

'Didn't you know?' Roberta obviously thought she did. 'I was such a pain—I'd never have been able to pull off the surprise if Barden hadn't—' She broke off, but, in as chatty a mood as Emmie had supposed, she resumed enthusiastically, 'I wanted to give Neville a surprise birthday party, the best birthday weekend he'd ever had. He was fifty,' she confided, 'and he was really down in the doldrums about it—I suppose I'll be the same when my fiftieth looms. Anyhow, as Neville works from home, I knew I didn't stand a cat in Hades' chance of it being a total surprise if I sent out the invitations. There were several terrifying moments when I thought he'd rumbled—Sarah Birch nearly blew it when she rang here instead of ringing Barden, but luckily I was able to point her in Barden's direction without Neville being any the wiser.'

'The—party—was a total surprise to your husband?' Emmie asked chokily, her husky tone having little to do with her cold this time.

'Absolutely,' Roberta replied, sounding positively cock-a-hoop. 'My dear, dear man was totally stunned. He had been expecting a quiet night at home, but one after the other our friends turned up.'

By the sound of it Roberta Short utterly adored her husband, and would no more think of taking a lover than she would kick a lame dog!

'I'm glad,' was the best Emmie could manage, while snippets of conversation—and her misinterpretation of them—whizzed around in her head.

'Oh, so am I. Neville said—' Suddenly Roberta halted. 'I'm keeping you from your work! I'm sorry. Everything went off so well, I can—' She broke off again. 'I'm going,' she said firmly. 'No need to tell Barden I rang; I'll ring him later when he's not so busy. Though Neville said he'd… I'm going,' she said again. 'Bye, Emmie.'

'Bye, Mrs Short,' Emmie replied—but found she was talking to herself.

Oh, Lord—she wanted to die. She sneezed—but her death wish had nothing to do with her cold. How crass! How impudent! Oh, heck, how absolutely everything! Barden wasn't having an affair with his friend's wife! By the sound of it—probably because he felt they must have had their fill of visitors now the weekend was over— Barden hadn't even called in on the Shorts last night, when he'd only been a short distance down the road.

Snatches of conversation thundered back. 'Neville mustn't know I'm phoning,' Roberta had said when she'd called. 'I've an idea he already suspects… He mustn't find out.' And Barden had told Roberta, 'Neville has no idea what you're up to.' Of course he hadn't—that was the *whole point* of a surprise party! 'He's not likely to divorce you,' Barden had confidently assured her. Why would Neville divorce his wife? What man would? Her only crime was to arrange a wonderful party to cheer him when he was feeling down about being fifty.

Never had Emmie felt more guilt-ridden as everything slotted into place. Even Barden's promise to have a few words with Roberta at the theatre last Thursday took on a different meaning. It had been no snatched meeting between two lovers. With all the arrangements in place for the following evening, it had merely been Barden attempting to assure a jittery Roberta that nothing was going to go wrong at the last minute. Which, by the sound of Roberta's euphoria just now, it hadn't.

Except, Emmie thought miserably, *she* had got it all wrong. Feeling down in the depths, she tried to find some justification for the way she had got it wrong. Barden Cunningham might not be having an affair, but he was, without question, a womaniser. Just look at all those women who rang him—and to whom he was charming. Claudia and Ingrid, she ticked off. Not to mention Paula, Sarah, and...

Sarah! Oh, no! Was there no end to her shame? Roberta Short's words came back to her. 'Sarah Birch nearly blew it when she rang here...' Oh, grief, were all those women friends of the Shorts, who had rung to confirm they would be at the party?

By the time Barden was free to take calls, Emmie wanted to run away and hide. It was no use telling herself that Barden should have denied he was having an affair that day when he'd clearly known what she was thinking. Why should he have denied it? Who was she but, she recalled painfully, some prissy little Miss Prim and Proper?

Emmie sneezed, shivered, for all the office was warm, and couldn't remember the last time she'd felt so thoroughly dejected. She was going to have to apologise, that was for sure!

She was still sneezing and rehearsing her apology when a short while later the connecting door opened and Barden strode in. He took one glance at her watery eyes and red-tipped nose, took a step back when she grabbed a tissue and sneezed—and then, as she looked across at him, he actually smiled.

It was the smile, Emmie rather supposed, that was responsible for sending all thought of making her apology clear out of her head. His words, as he rocked back on his heels to study her, were not conducive to allowing her to recall that she had something she should be sorry for.

'Well, well, little Nellie-know-it-all, I thought you couldn't catch cold from getting frozen and wet. I thought it was a scientific fact that—'

'There's a virus going round!' she butted in—huskily, and with far more authority than her lie should have allowed.

Barden came nearer, 'You're going home!' he decreed, his authority beating hers into a cocked hat.

'No, I'm not!' she spluttered. But as again she sneezed he was getting her coat and was holding it out for her to put her arms in. 'I've too much to do,' she protested, not moving an inch.

'Am I wrong, or am I wrong?' Barden enquired smoothly. 'Do you really want to give Dawn—who already has more than enough problems in her pregnancy—a heavy cold to go with them?'

Pig! Emmie fumed, but stood up. 'Messages,' she muttered grumpily, pointing to her notepad. She had recorded that Roberta Short had phoned but had left no message. Emmie was not, as she put her arms into her coat, which Barden continued to hold out for her, in any mood to apologise for anything. Then she forgot everything as a thrill of a tingle went through the whole of her body when Barden's fingers had touched her neck as he'd pulled her hair away from her collar.

'You're burning up!' he stated as she jerked from him, not a sign of a smile about him. 'Are you all right to drive?'

'I've a cold, not pneumonia!'

'Make sure you don't get it!' he threatened. 'I don't want your pneumonia on my conscience.'

Emmie looked at him—he'd nothing on his conscience, she realised. Her apology hovered—'Barden, I...' Hastily she grabbed for a tissue and sneezed.

'Go home and get into bed—and stay there!' he ordered.

Suddenly it seemed the best idea she'd heard in a long while. She went.

Emmie spent the rest of the day in bed and awakened on Wednesday, accepting that she had a streaming cold but knowing that but for Dawn she would have left her bed and gone to the office.

She stayed home and rang Aunt Hannah and had a long, if occasionally slightly weird, chat with her. Adrian popped down to see her that evening, but didn't stay—he didn't want her cold and she didn't want company.

Dawn phoned her on Thursday to ask how she was feeling. By then Emmie's husky voice had turned into a croak. 'Don't try talking; I can hear how you are,' Dawn sympathised.

'How are you?' Emmie croaked.

'Believe me—much better than you,' Dawn assured her, and rang off.

Not long afterwards the phone rang again. 'Do you need a doctor?' Barden Cunningham asked without preamble.

'Good heavens, no!' Emmie exclaimed, while her heart started to thunder quite unnecessarily. 'I should be embarrassed to death!' she stated firmly, if croakily, a sneeze imminent.

'You sound like hell!'

'I look terrific!'

He rang off without another word. Emmie put her phone down and snuggled beneath the covers. She looked a wreck and she knew it. She closed her eyes, coughed, sneezed, and sat up in bed. She felt as if she could sleep for a week—but the cough she'd developed decreed otherwise.

Around an hour later her doorbell sounded. She was of half a mind not to answer it. It rang again. Emmie got out of bed, wrapped a silk robe around her, and went to the front door.

Her face was already flushed; she flushed some more. 'You lied!' Barden Cunningham said. So, okay, she didn't look terrific. She turned her back on him and went to her sitting room. Barden followed. 'Sit down before you fall down,' he ordered, and placed the various packages he was carrying down on a low table. 'I called in at the pharmacy,' he commented—and Emmie suddenly felt quite weepy.

'It's ages since—' She broke off, swallowing hard.

'Since?' he enquired, coming to join her on the sofa. Emmie shook her tousled head. 'Since—anyone last looked after you?' he suggested gently.

'I'm being feeble,' she commented, striving for a bright note.

Barden studied her for a moment, and then teased, 'Let me make the most of it. You're usually rearing up at me for something.'

'Oh, Barden,' she mourned regretfully. 'I owe you an apology.'

'What did you do?'

'You never did—were never having an affair with Roberta Short. I...' She swallowed on a sore throat. 'I should never have thought what I did. When Mrs Short phoned on Monday she referred to your part in her surprise party for her husband—and I feel dreadful.'

'You choose your moments!' Barden replied. 'Any other time I'd probably have had a few words with you on the subject of jumping to conclusions—let alone what the devil it's got to do with you. But look at you, all huge-eyed and with the very latest in pretty pink-tipped noses. Who could be angry with you?'

'You're more kind than I deserve,' she told him painfully.

'Steady! You'll be going into compliment mode if you aren't careful.' Emmie giggled, and Barden shook his head, 'How the blazes you manage to sound all giggly-girlish and incredibly sexy at the same time defeats me,' he stated.

'Blame it on my husky throat,' she laughed, and found herself adding, 'Am I light-headed?'

'Do you feel light-headed?'

'I feel—as though I—like you.'

Barden stared at her for some long, hard moments. Then all at once he smiled. 'I should bring you cough linctus more often,' he said, and stood up, asking, 'What are you doing for food?'

'I've plenty in,' she answered. 'Aunt Hannah and I make things for the freezer most weekends.'

'Be good,' he bade her, and let himself out.

He was in her head for the rest of the day. And there again when she awoke, feeling much better, the next morning. His kindness in bringing medication to soothe her throat, and a couple of other remedies, touched her greatly. She did so appreciate that, when in receipt of her apology, he hadn't blasted her ears for her audacity in daring to think what she had about something that was nothing to do with her anyway.

Emmie still had Barden popping into her head off and on when, early that evening, he telephoned her. 'How's my second-best PA?' he enquired.

'How good of you to ring!' she exclaimed, never stopping to wonder why she should be so exceedingly pleased to hear him. Had she really told him she liked him?

'You're sounding better.'

'Oh, I am. I'll be back at the office on Monday.'

'Only if you feel up to it,' he declared. 'And you'll have to take it quietly this weekend.'

'Yes, Doctor,' she smiled.

'You haven't got a madcap weekend planned, I trust?'

Was that a threatening note she detected? Well, she had just had nearly four days away from his office, so she supposed he was entitled to want her not to do anything that might prevent her from being fully fit come Monday.

'Nothing too madcap,' she agreed, and found herself confiding, 'I had planned to drive Aunt Hannah to the National Motorcycle Museum in Birmingham tomorrow.'

'You're not fit yet!' Barden objected.

Any other time Emmie might have been nettled by his attitude. She guessed her cold must have taken more out of her than she realised. 'I'm a bit concerned I may still be a little infectious,' she admitted. 'Though Aunt Hannah would have it that she and the rest of the elderly residents at Keswick House have lived long enough now to have built up a powerful immunity to the common cold.'

'But you're worried you may pass your germs on to the residents if you call there for her?'

'I suppose I could send a taxi for her,' Emmie considered.

'You realise, of course, that all the way to Birmingham your germs will be bouncing around the close confines of your car.'

He made it sound monstrous. 'Perhaps I'd better leave the trip until next week.' She reluctantly saw sense.

'A much better idea.'

'I can still have Aunt Hannah here with me, though. Still send a taxi for...'

'Why don't I go and see her?'

Astonished, Emmie was lost for words for a moment. 'I can't let you do that!' was her first reaction. Followed by, 'Why would you?'

'Because my very conscientious PA is getting all uptight about checking on her step-relative to see how she is after her adventurous episode last Monday, and because I happen to be passing that way tomorrow and also happen to have a free half-hour.'

'But—I couldn't allow...' Emmie began to protest.

'And also because Mrs Whitford invited me, only last Monday, to drop in for a cup of tea whenever I was passing.'

'Yes, but...'

'How can you argue?' There was a smile in his voice.

'It's in my nature. I must be getting better.'

'Keep warm,' he ordered, 'It's bitterly cold out,' and, so saying, he rang off, and Emmie became quite dreamy about him.

Emmie had recovered by Saturday morning, but when she rang Aunt Hannah the sweet love wouldn't hear of Emmie taking her anywhere. 'You haven't been well, and besides, we've got some entertainment here tonight. Amateurs, of course, but since they've kindly given up their free time to come and sing to us, it seems only polite to stay and listen to them.'

'Barden Cunningham, my *boss*,' Emmie emphasised, lest Aunt Hannah was still carrying the notion that Barden was her fiancé, 'may call and see you some time today.'

'That will be nice,' Aunt Hannah replied. And to prove her memory was as good as ever, she went on, 'I invited him to do that whenever he was passing.'

Emmie felt very much cheered after her phone call. She felt so much better, and her appetite suddenly returned, so she decided a walk to the corner shop to buy some fresh fruit, vegetables and milk would do her good.

As Barden had said last evening, it was bitterly cold out. She was glad to return to her flat to get warmed through again. She played with the idea in the late afternoon of phoning Aunt Hannah to enquire if Barden had called.

She decided against it, but found she could barely wait until she thought her step-relative would be up and on the move the next morning to ring her. When she did call, however, she received one almighty shock.

'Did Barden Cunningham call yesterday?' she asked, after their initial chat was over.

'Oh, yes, we had a most wonderful day!' Aunt Hannah informed her enthusiastically.

For a second or two Emmie feared her step-grandmother's memory was throwing another wobbly. 'Day?' she queried gently. 'Um, did you...did he stay for coffee or tea?'

'Oh, we didn't have time when he called!' Aunt Hannah replied. 'We had coffee on the way and lunch when we got there. Did you know his father is a classic car enthusiast and has several of them?'

Emmie didn't, but by then she was starting to grow seriously worried. 'Where—er—did you have lunch?' she probed casually.

'The museum.'

'The museum,' Emmie echoed faintly. 'The Motorcycle Museum?' Surely not?

'Of course. Oh, it was wonderful! Lovely!' Aunt Hannah went on and into raptures about the motorcycles she'd seen.

Emmie was utterly stunned, and came away from the phone not knowing what to believe. Feeling quite free of her cold now, her sore throat gone, she had intended to invite Aunt Hannah to lunch. But all that had gone out of her head and she collapsed into a chair. Had Barden *really* taken Aunt Hannah to the Motorcycle Museum yesterday? Or, having set her mind on going yesterday, had the dear soul imagined it?

Having thawed out food from the freezer, Emmie set it to cook with her mind in a chaotic whirl. She knew Barden's home number—should she give him a ring? She felt worried enough to do so, while at the same time she also felt an unaccountable overwhelming shyness about doing anything of the sort.

She went to the phone several times, but it was only when she began to see that the very plain likelihood was that Aunt Hannah had imagined her trip, and she was going to have to get some specialised help for her—and soon—that she went and dialled Barden's number.

It rang and rang—he wasn't in. Emmie replaced the phone and didn't like at all the images that came to mind of him out at lunch somewhere, with a Claudia, or Paula, Sarah or Ingrid. What on earth was the matter with her? Good grief!

Deciding she'd had too much time on her hands just lately, Emmie went and peeled some potatoes and put them on to boil. She next attended to the broccoli—and then the doorbell sounded.

Her thoughts went immediately to Aunt Hannah, and she rushed to the outer door—to discover that this was her day for shocks. Barden Cunningham stood there.

She opened her mouth, and closed it. He got in first. 'Up and dressed, I see,' he observed.

'I've just tried to ring you.'

'Happens all the time,' he replied, and Emmie felt just a touch ruffled. Clearly he expected women to ring him a lot, and he didn't seem bothered as to why she would try to ring him anyway. 'Something smells good,' he commented, sniffing the air.

She felt perverse. 'You wouldn't enjoy it.'

'Are you always this mean?'

'So stay to lunch!' she invited snappily—and nearly dropped to the floor when, by stepping over the threshold, he accepted.

She left him in the sitting room while she went and checked the boiling potatoes. It didn't surprise her that she had peeled more than enough for two—her brain just wasn't engaged that morning.

A sound behind her made her turn. 'So tell me?' he invited.

Why she had tried to phone him. Now that they were face to face, there in person, it seemed ridiculous to ask if he had taken Aunt Hannah to Birmingham yesterday. Of course he hadn't! Yet, remembering how pleasant he had been to Aunt Hannah on Monday, and his offer to call and see the old lady yesterday—notwithstanding his kindness to Emmie herself in calling on Thursday with medication, she reflected—she began to waver in her certainty that he hadn't taken Aunt Hannah out yesterday. He *was* kind— but could he be *extraordinarily* kind?

'Did you…?' She couldn't get it out. 'I rang Aunt Hannah this morning.'

'She's nowhere near as mixed-up as I first supposed,' Barden remarked affably, his grey eyes fixed on Emmie's slightly anxious brown ones. 'You're looking better,' he threw in. 'Restored to full beauty.'

She was sidetracked. Was he teasing? She wanted him to think her beautiful. 'It's a gift,' she said, pulling herself together. 'Did you call at Keswick House yesterday?'

'I said I would.'

'By the sound of it, you—um—had an intelligent conversation with my step-grandmother?'

'Mrs Whitford seldom seemed stuck for words,' he answered tactfully of Emmie's sometimes garrulous relation.

'Er—how long were you with her?'

Barden studied her and, while Emmie was beating all around the bush, he, as she knew, was never one to dodge anything. 'She enjoyed it,' he stated.

'Oh, Barden, no! You didn't?'

'I did,' he confirmed. 'I enjoyed it too.'

Emmie finished bush-beating. 'You took Aunt Hannah to Birmingham?'

'It seemed a shame to disappoint her,' he replied, and suddenly Emmie had the most horrendous thought.

'Aunt Hannah thought that was why you called yesterday, didn't she?'

'You've gone pink,' he observed.

'I'm going to die of embarrassment!'

'Not you!' he declared. 'What are we having for lunch?'

Emmie wasn't so easily deflected. 'Just a minute. You called in at Keswick House, intending to stay only a half-hour at the outside, but instead when Aunt…'

'I've told you, I enjoyed it. The dear lady's technical knowledge is astonishing.' He took a glance at the glass-fronted oven. 'Are you doing Yorkshire puddings to go with that beef?'

She would have prepared some had Aunt Hannah been there, but it was too late now. She shook her head. 'You'll have to fill up on apple pie afterwards.'

Oddly, because Barden was her employer, not to mention the fact that he had more or less invited himself to lunch, Emmie would not have been a bit surprised had lunch been a stilted kind of affair. But not a bit of it. Barden had a wealth of charm, as she well knew, for all it was seldom directed at her. During the meal his manner was easy, charming and, save for her briefly mentioning the two-week working trip to the States he was to undertake in a fortnight's time, work was never discussed.

What was raised, though, was her family background. 'Your father was a scientist?' Barden enquired at one point.

Aunt Hannah had been talking! 'Your father has several classic cars,' Emmie countered—and loved it when Barden laughed.

'Do you remember your father?' he enquired softly a few moments later. 'You were ten when he died, you mentioned?'

Emmie gave in. 'My father was a gentle man—quiet, often preoccupied, but always there for me.'

'As was your stepfather.' It was a statement.

Emmie smiled, 'Alec was lovely. Exactly the opposite of my father, though.'

'Not so often preoccupied?' Barden suggested, and she wondered just how much Aunt Hannah had told him.

'He was fun.'

'What work did he do?'

Ah! 'He—um—was always busy,' Emmie prevaricated.

'He liked to gamble. Don't get uptight!' Barden instructed. 'I didn't ask. Mrs Whitford said she hadn't had a decent conversation for days, and chatted about anything that came to her on the way to Birmingham.'

'It was all motorcycles on the way back?' Emmie guessed.

'That and classic cars.' Emmie thought they had left behind talk of her family—but she should have known better. Didn't she know all about his 'dog with a bone' tenacity for finding out what he wanted to know? 'According to Mrs Whitford, her son sold many of your mother's antiques over the years.'

'We've still got a few pieces left,' she defended. 'And we've always managed...'

'I've an idea you always will manage, won't you, Emmie?' Barden said, his tone kindly. She wasn't sure she knew what he was getting at, and realised her uncertainty must have shown when he went on, 'You moved from a very comfortable area when needs dictated.'

Needs dictated? You could say that. 'Security, financial security, mine and Aunt Hannah's, has to be my first and highest priority,' Emmie admitted.

'You moved because you could no longer afford to live where you were—not when Mrs Whitford had moved into residential care.'

'She's free at Keswick House to come and go as she pleases,' Emmie told him.

'Provided she tells someone where she's going,' he put in—well, he had proof of that, didn't he?—and also proof that Aunt Hannah sometimes liked to bend the rules.

'It's important that Aunt Hannah feels safe,' Emmie revealed slowly. Barden knew so much, there seemed little point in pretending that matters were other than how they were.

'Was she not safe before?'

'I have to go to work—I like going to work,' she inserted, lest he should run away with the idea that she hated working in his office. 'But if I work it means I have to leave her on her own for too long for five days a week. Rather belatedly I saw, when Aunt Hannah had her first bout of being a little confused, that the dear love would be happier if she had company during the day.'

'So, to keep your financial security, you moved to some-where cheaper to r—'

'You make it sound like some tremendous sacrifice.' Emmie smiled. 'But it wasn't. Aunt Hannah pays the lion's share of living at Keswick House, and I can't say that the value I put on my financial security is anything new.'

'It isn't?'

Emmie felt she had said more than enough. 'It isn't,' she confirmed, and, the subject closed, prepared to collect up their pudding plates.

'When did it start?' he wanted to know.

'Do you never give up?' she asked exasperatedly.

'What do you think?' He grinned, such charm in his expression that she found herself actually thinking back and trying to remember when she had started to value her fi-nancial security so much.

'There was a point after Alec died when I realised the only family I had was Aunt Hannah, and that there was no one else to look after us. But, with dear Alec being the way he was, I probably felt the first threat to my security when he sold the house and...'

'It was his to sell?'

'It was when my mother died.'

'Oh, Emmie,' Barden said softly.

'What does that mean?'

'No wonder you're down on men.'

Her eyes widened. She stood up and busied herself with the dishes. 'I'm not down on men at all!' she denied, and found that Barden was on his feet too and was coming over.

'When did you last allow any man to kiss you?' he asked—just as if that was evidence that she didn't have a down on men!

'If memory serves—just last Monday!' she answered.

'Who?' he demanded.

'I see I left an indelible impression,' she smirked.

And knew he'd realised that *he* had been the man who

had last kissed her when he asked, 'You're sure you're no longer infectious?' A smile was there in his voice somewhere.

'Positive,' she replied.

And got the shock of her life when, taking the dishes from her and putting them back on the table, Barden then gathered her in his arms and, while her heart started to go like a trip-hammer, he murmured, 'I'll risk it,' and, his head coming down, he kissed her, tenderly, but thoroughly.

Emmie was fairly speechless when that wonderfully tender kiss ended. 'If—er—if that was a—um—thank-you for your lunch, you needn't hang around to do the washing up,' she told him huskily, giving herself a slight push away from him.

Barden let her go, his arms dropping to his sides. 'What sort of a cad do you think I am?' he growled, and she laughed, and they washed up together. But she was glad when, all chores done, he went—her legs had never felt more wobbly.

Emmie returned to work on Monday, having been fully able to convince herself that the only reason she had felt her legs go weak yesterday was because she hadn't been terribly well. She had trouble convincing herself that her heart didn't give a bit of a flutter when she first saw Barden that day, though.

He greeted her in friendly fashion, but was no more friendly to her than he was to anyone else. She was in his office later that morning when her eyes strayed to his rather superb mouth—those lips that had gently kissed hers yesterday. Hastily she flicked her glance from his mouth to his eyes—and saw that his glance was on her mouth.

Abruptly he turned his attention to the work on his desk. 'It looks as if I'll have to be in Stratford Thursday afternoon. I'll need you with me.'

'Fine,' she answered, aware that as well as telling her that they'd probably be back late he was also assuming that she wouldn't have any problem with that. And so a busy week got under way.

Emmie joined Adrian up at his flat for a meal on Tuesday. She liked him, but there was never any suggestion that they might be more than friends. She guessed that, as she felt safe with him, Adrian felt safe with her.

On Wednesday evening Emmie had a long telephone conversation with Aunt Hannah, who asked if she would mind if she didn't see her this Saturday as she and Mrs Vellacott were going to a play that one of the local schools was performing on Saturday evening.

'How are you getting there?' Emmie questioned, not happy at the thought of her step-grandmother walking the streets after dark.

'Mrs Vellacott's son-in-law is picking us up and bringing us back,' Aunt Hannah assured her.

'You'll come and have lunch with me on Sunday?' Emmie asked, and could only be pleased that Aunt Hannah seemed to be having more of a social life these days.

'I'm looking forward to it,' Aunt Hannah declared, and asked, 'How's Barden? Have you seen him this week?' Oh, dear, had she forgotten he was her employer?

'I work for him; I see him every day,' Emmie said carefully.

'Of course you do. What am I thinking of?' There was a pause and then, wickedly, 'He's rather dishy, isn't he? Oh, to be sixty years younger!'

'You're incorrigible!'

'Too late to change now. He's definitely got that certain something, though, that—without him having to lift a finger—has women falling all over him.'

Emmie went to bed that night determined that that was one club she wasn't going to join. And got up the next morning wondering what on earth she had been thinking about. Good heavens, of course she wasn't going to join

Barden Cunningham's fan club. The whole idea was pre-
posterous.

She went to work realising that she had been feeling very
unsettled since last Sunday when, so tenderly, Barden had
gathered her into his arms and kissed her. Why he had was
a trifle confusing. Probably it was some male ego thing,
because he thought she didn't allow any man to kiss her.
Though—it hadn't seemed like that. Truth to tell, it had
been rather a lovely...

Pfff—she'd take jolly good care he didn't kiss her again.
Not that he seemed remotely interested in doing so. If the
one-sided conversation she overheard that morning, when
he was on the phone to some female named Karla Nesbitt,
was anything to go by, Barden Cunningham Esquire had
other things on his mind than kissing his assistant acting
PA.

They started out for Stratford-upon-Avon at two and
managed to get there by four. Barden seemed preoccupied
on the journey, his thoughts either on work or the date he'd
arranged with the sultry-sounding Karla Nesbitt. He was
taking her out somewhere tomorrow evening.

They finished their business in Stratford at six-thirty, and
Jack Bryant walked with them to Barden's car. But it was
to Emmie's side of the car that he came, and, in an under-
tone, he informed her warmly, 'My divorce becomes absolute in two weeks.'

'Congratulations,' Emmie replied.

'What I'm telling you is that I'll be free in two weeks—
a single man. I thought—'

Barden's voice, a touch impatient cut through what else
Jack had to say. 'I wouldn't mind getting back to London
before midnight!' he stated shortly.

What a pig! What an embarrassing pig! Trying to make
her look small! 'Bye, Jack,' Emmie smiled, and only just
stopped herself from inviting him to give her a call when
the two weeks were up. She got into the car realising that,

though she liked Jack Bryant, she didn't know that she wanted to go out with him.

'What was Bryant talking to you about?' Barden asked curtly.

'He was telling me the state of his divorce,' she answered coolly.

She was, by then, not feeling very friendly towards her employer, and when fifteen minutes later he—in her opinion—begrudgingly enquired, 'Do you want to stop for something to eat?' Emmie knew she'd sooner starve.

'Do you mind if we get on? I'm seeing someone later tonight.' Charming! His foot went down on the accelerator and they nearly took off at the sudden surge of power!

He remembered his manners, though, when they reached her flat, and Emmie, having calmed down somewhat, was prepared to give a few plus-marks because he got out of his car with her and took her door keys from her.

Unfortunately, probably in his haste to be away, Barden collected an over-large splinter from the splitting door-post—and in attempting to hurriedly extract it succeeded only in breaking it off, leaving part of the wood under the skin of his index finger.

Automatically Emmie took a hold of his hand. 'Have you got a nanny at home?' she enquired lightly.

'Are you being funny?'

She'd had it with him! It had been a long day—and they were still all too obviously not the best of friends. 'Apparently not,' she answered a touch waspishly. 'You'd better come in; I can't see a thing in this light.' She hoped it hurt!

She had expected, out of sheer perversity, that he'd decline her offer in no uncertain terms. But, rather to her surprise, he kept a hold of her keys and crossed the hall to open up her flat.

'I won't be a moment,' she informed him and, draping her car coat over the sofa, she left him in the sitting room while she went to collect her tweezers. She returned with a surgical-spirit-sterilised needle and took a hold of his hand again, to inspect the damage. 'It won't hurt half as much if you don't look,' she promised him, suddenly very ashamed of her hope that his finger hurt.

'Do I get a sweetie if I don't cry out?' he asked—and Emmie folded, her good humour back. The remains of the splinter came out cleanly—and, oh, she did so love him. *Love him?*

Her head jerked up—just as he lowered his head to inspect her handiwork. Their heads touched, then jerked away. Then suddenly, and she had no idea which of them had moved first, they were closer, his hands were reaching for her, and she again knew the bliss of being in his arms.

His kiss, when his lips met hers, was as tender as it had been on Sunday. But where on Sunday Barden had held her firmly, but not too closely, this time his arms seemed to be compelling her forward.

Emmie moved that little bit closer, and Barden kissed her again, his kiss deeper and gentler still, but starting to seek, seek, take and give. And all at once there was a fire flickering into life inside her. Emmie put her arms around him under his jacket; she wanted to be closer—she had never been in love before. His body, the warmth of him through his fine shirt, was dizzying. She had never imagined that to stand this close, to feel, to touch, while at the same time being held secure in the all-male arms of the man she loved, could be so utterly enthralling.

Then it seemed that to feel and to touch was not all one-sided. For, as though wanting to feel her warmth too, she sensed Barden's hands come beneath her jacket, and was mindless for ageless seconds as he caressed up to her ribcage over the thin silk of her shirt.

He kissed her again deeply, and their bodies touched. He kissed her throat while, in a tender whisper of a caress, his hands moved on upwards. To Emmie, when she felt his hands cup her full breasts, felt his fingers tantalising the hardened firm tips, it was an experience like no other.

Which made it a mystery to her that, when in his arms was where she wanted to be, she should then, at that utterly blissful moment, strangle out the one word, 'Don't.' He stilled immediately. 'Don't, Barden,' she found from a reluctant somewhere.

He took his hands from her breasts, moved them to hold her by her waist, and raised his head to look down at her. Emmie couldn't take his scrutiny. She turned abruptly about, presenting him with her back—and had to swallow hard when she felt his hands leave her waist as he caught hold of her by her shoulders.

'That—wasn't supposed to happen,' he said in her ear—and Emmie knew then that he was already regretting it.

'It—didn't,' she answered, grateful for pride's helping hand.

'Are you all right?' he questioned gruffly.

No, she was not all right! She had just discovered that she loved him, was in love with him, and she knew that when she was alone, when he had gone, her love was going to start to hurt.

'Good heavens, yes,' she assured him lightly—but had to move a few steps until she was away from his tingling, yearning-making hold.

She heard him move, and fought desperately to breathe normally. Then realised that he had taken her at her word that she was all right, for the next sound she heard was the sound of the sitting room door closing as Barden let himself out of her flat. All right? Nothing was ever going to be all right ever again!

CHAPTER SIX

WITH the coming of the cold light of day, Emmie found that her love for Barden was no figment of her imagination. She got out of bed and supposed she must have had a few hours' sleep. It didn't feel like it.

She stood under the shower with the same realisations tormenting her that had tormented her through the night. She was in love with him, and in all honesty now knew that it had been coming on since the first time she met him.

Emmie no longer wondered what had happened to her certainty of only yesterday morning, that she'd take jolly good care Barden didn't kiss her again. He had only had to reach for her—and that certainty had caved in.

What would have happened had not some semblance of sanity panicked her into telling him 'Don't', she didn't want to consider. Barden had shown no sign of being the one to end the interlude, that was for sure.

Emmie left her bathroom no nearer to finding an explanation for why she had fallen in love with him. Perhaps there wasn't an explanation for loving someone you didn't want to love—she was going to find no joy in it; she knew that. She loved him, and that love was here to stay, was unshakeable. But Barden did not love her, she had to face up to that, nor was it possible that he ever would.

What could be explained now, though, were those tiny little pointers along the way—overlooked then, significant today. For instance, that sensation of feeling oddly let down, upset when—and it happened a lot, as she well knew—she had believed he was having an affair with his friend's wife.

Emmie recalled, too, how she hadn't liked it when she'd

thought he was a womaniser. Well, she had been proved wrong there. Or had she? He might not have been lusting after *mesdames* Ingrid, Paula and Co, but he wasn't staying home nights, was he? She knew for a fact he would be out with Karla Nesbitt tonight.

Jealousy, cruel, spiteful jealousy, nipped, and Emmie drove herself to work determining she was going to overcome it—as she was going to overcome her love for Barden. She'd get herself a social life. Everyone had one bar her—well, there was Adrian. Even Aunt Hannah had a better social life than she did. Emmie decided right then that there was nothing to stop her from going out once in a while. And she would! In fact she'd go out with the very next person who asked her.

In remembering Aunt Hannah, though, Emmie had to wonder if *that* was the reason why when, close to Barden, and experiencing such wild and wonderful emotions, emotions such as she had never experienced before, she had found that awful word 'don't'. Had her subconscious been battering at her even then, while she had been thrilling to Barden's touch? Had her subconscious been alerting her to the fact that she mustn't let herself be another of Barden's women because, should they ever indulge in any sort of an affair, when it ended there was every probability that her job would end with it too?

Her security, and that of Aunt Hannah, was still paramount, Emmie mused disconsolately as she parked her car and made for her office. Not that Barden had done much more than kiss her—so that hardly meant he wanted a full-blown affair. But he was a man of the world—and she couldn't take that risk.

'Good morning,' she greeted Dawn cheerfully, pleased to see that her colleague was looking better than she had of late.

Barden came in to their office long before Emmie was ready to see him again. When would she ever be ready to see him again? She managed to meet his eyes, but felt his glance taking in her blush. 'If you'd bring through your notes from Stratford,' he suggested, and from there it was all work.

Emmie returned to her desk feeling very much anti the man she loved. Do this, do that—you'd never have known that less than twenty-four hours ago he had kissed her, laid so much as a finger on her, so impersonal was he. She hoped she hadn't got all of the splinter out—hoped that his finger turned septic.

She was, of course, hating herself for thinking anything so disgraceful by the time it came for her to go home. He was good and kind and had overturned a lot of her earlier not-so-nice opinions of him—and now she wouldn't see him for *two whole days*. It was unbearable.

With a very bleak weekend stretching before her, Emmie made her way to the car park, only to be waylaid by Simon Elsworth, one of the management trainees whom she knew slightly and who had obviously been hanging around waiting for her.

'I wondered if you'd like to come out to dinner with me?' he asked, and Emmie's determination to get herself a social life abruptly disintegrated. He wasn't Barden.

'I—er—I'm a little busy this weekend.' She tried to let him down gently.

'It doesn't have to be this weekend,' Simon said eagerly. 'How about next Tuesday?'

Emmie searched for tact, then remembered how Mr I-don't-even-remember-kissing-you Cunningham was dating all and sundry—well, she knew about Karla Nesbitt for a fact. 'I think I should like that,' she answered.

She was regretting having agreed to go out with Simon before she had so much as made it out of the car park, though Simon was soon gone from her mind.

With a long, long day stretching before her, Emmie got up on Saturday and decided that she wasn't going to waste another minute in thinking about Barden. Easier said than done. To keep herself occupied she cleaned and polished, had a brief respite when Adrian came down and cadged a cup of coffee, then stripped beds and remade them, washed and baked, then, physically tired, but mentally alert, she had a soak in the bath and went to bed.

But, as tired as she felt, Emmie found she couldn't sleep. She would not, not, not, not, *not* think about *him*! She picked up her current book and opened it, but, absorbed in thoughts of Barden, was suddenly startled when her door-bell rang.

Aunt Hannah! A hurried glance at her bedside clock showed eleven-forty. Worried that Aunt Hannah might have decided not to wait until she was collected tomorrow, Emmie quickly pulled on her silk robe and dashed to answer the door.

It was not, however, Aunt Hannah who stood there when Emmie pulled back the door, but, to her utter astonishment, Barden Cunningham! He had on a lounge suit, shirt and tie, and while her mouth fell open, so her heart went wild.

Speechlessly she stared at him, which made it just as well that he was the first to speak. 'I'm starting with a migraine,' he explained. 'I don't think I'm going to make it home before my vision's affected.'

Oh, my poor darling! Instantly Emmie went into action. He was, she realised, not the best colour she had ever seen. 'You do look a bit green around the gills,' she murmured, striving to hide her sudden agitation at seeing him so stricken. 'Come in.'

He appeared to make automatically for her sitting room while she secured the outer door. 'If I could borrow a chair for a while?' he asked, seeming to notice only then that she was in her night attire.

'You look as if you'd be better lying down than standing up!' It was decision time, only the decision was already made for her. She had never expected to see him so vulnerable, and her heart ached. She had once shared a bedroom with him and not come to the slightest harm. Poor darling. It wouldn't come to that, he could have a room to himself. 'Luckily for you Aunt Hannah's bed's made up.'

'She's not with you this weekend?'

'You're swaying!' Emmie took charge. 'Come on,' she said, but guessed he was having trouble focusing and did the only thing possible. 'This way,' she said, more gently, and caught a hold of his right arm and led him into Aunt Hannah's room. 'Have you been able to take anything for it?' she asked as she guided him to sit on the bed.

'I don't get cursed this way that often to need to carry medication, but I'll take anything you've got,' he answered. Emmie, who had an idea from somewhere that once a migraine got started it was too late to take medication, went quickly all the same to get him painkillers and some water.

'Have you had much to drink?' she thought to ask, before she handed the tablets over.

'A glass of something red and foul enough for me to refuse a second.'

Emmie didn't know much about it but wondered briefly if the foul red wine had triggered his migraine attack. She handed a couple of tablets over, and waited while he downed them. 'It doesn't sound as if it was too scintillating an evening,' she commented, taking the glass of water from him.

'A party,' he answered briefly, and she could tell he was having a problem in concentrating, though he added, 'I was driving near here on my way home when I realised I was in trouble.'

'Don't talk any more.' Emmie shushed him, and bent to remove his shoes and socks. Then, straightening, she went to help him out of his jacket. She could tell that he was really suffering when, his eyes closed, all movement seemed painful to him.

His eyes were still shut when she held him to her as,

almost unaided, she removed his jacket. She felt the side of his face against the swell of her breasts, and belatedly became aware that her robe had gaped open as she bent over him.

She held on to him, but very nearly let go of him when, almost into her breasts, he commented wearily, 'I trust you aren't planning to have your wicked way with me.'

Emmie smiled—dead, but refusing to stay down! A feeling of utter love and tenderness for him engulfed her, and she placed a whisper of a kiss on the top of his head. Then, with an arm around his shoulders, she managed to remove his tie.

Emmie wondered about removing his shirt, but felt he would prefer to be left alone. 'Lie down,' she instructed softly, and when he complied she settled for unfastening the buttons on his shirt. She also undid the waistband of his trousers. If he felt better shortly, it would not be too troublesome for him to take the remainder of his clothes off.

Emmie pulled the duvet up around him, and had just laid a cooling hand on his head when she saw that he had his eyes open. 'Kiss me, Emmie,' he requested, but sounded drained of energy.

Oh, she loved him, loved him! 'Promise you're harmless?'

'For the moment,' he answered.

'Sounds encouraging,' she teased, and because she wanted to she bent closer and, as he closed his eyes, she tenderly kissed him.

'Goodnight,' he murmured, and Emmie straightened, seeing that he didn't look any better. But, since he still had his eyes closed, she hoped he might drop off into pain-relieving sleep.

Emmie stayed only long enough to hang his jacket over the back of a chair, then, putting the light out as she went, she silently left the room.

She went back to bed, hoping that he would get some rest, some sleep. She couldn't. She admitted she liked having him so close. He hadn't been out with some female, then? Or had he? Had he just taken his date home when he'd felt the first vicious nip of migraine? A female who lived in this area?

Unable to settle to sleep, Emmie got out of bed and tiptoed to the next-door room. She had closed his door, and didn't want to disturb him if he had managed to fall asleep, so she listened, but heard no sound.

She returned to her bed, her ears attuned for any noises, but none came, and around four o'clock she finally succumbed to sleep.

It did not surprise her that she slept later than she normally did on a Sunday morning. What did surprise her was to awake and find the man she loved in her room.

As Emmie had assumed he might, Barden had removed the rest of his clothes and was now somewhat incongruously clad in the spare robe Aunt Hannah kept on a door hook. Emmie, her black shiny hair all over the place, struggled to sit up, while noticing that the robe, with its sleeves halfway up his arms, was far from a perfect fit. Her eyes travelled down to his bare feet, and then up past his quite handsome legs, his knees just covered, and on up to his face—more healthily complexioned this morning.

More because she was overly conscious of her tousled hair and feeling suddenly shy rather than because she needed an answer, she asked, 'How are you feeling?' She was able to see for herself that he looked fully fit again this morning.

His answer initially was to let his gaze travel slowly over her sleep-mussed hair and her pinkened complexion. Then he smiled, that leg-weakening smile, and answered, 'Never better.' And, leaning casually against a solid chest of drawers, he continued, 'Though...' He hesitated.

'Though?' she prompted slowly, her senses somehow alert for mischief.

'Though I think it's possible I've just ruined your love-life.'

He didn't, Emmie noticed, look devastatedly worried about that. 'Oh?' she queried warily, as yet without an inkling as to what he could mean.

'Know anybody by the name of Adrian?' he enquired nicely.

He knew full well she did. But—all sorts of clicks were clicking! It was not unknown for Adrian to come down to borrow something or other as soon as he thought she was up on a Sunday morning—or any other morning for that matter—be it milk, sugar or yesterday's paper.

Her eyes did a more detailed study of the tall, all-masculine, bristly-chinned man, his arms shooting out from the fit-where-it-touched robe, and his bare feet, bare, strong legs.

'You answered the door—looking like that?'

'I thought you'd want me to put on a robe,' he answered pleasantly, confirmation there, she realised, that he probably hadn't a stitch on underneath!

'You realise you've just ruined my reputation?' she told him severely, to hide how wonderful it was to see him; she had thought she would have to wait until tomorrow for a glimpse of him.

Barden stared back at her for long seconds, then mockingly drawled, 'You're not suggesting I marry you?'

And that made her mad. Clearly she was the very last person he would ever consider marrying! Who did she think he was? 'You should be so lucky!' she flared. She wouldn't marry him if he asked her—oh, to have the chance! 'You've obviously recovered,' she snapped. 'Let yourself out!'

'I'm not allowed to stay for breakfast?'

'Make it a first!' she erupted—but, crazy as it was, from having just fumed, she now had to laugh.

Barden stilled, his glance on her happy face and merry eyes. Then abruptly he moved from the chest of drawers and took a few steps to the doorway. Then, however, he turned, and suddenly his eyes were filled with devilment when he said, 'Permit me to tell you, Miss Lawson, that you have an exceedingly snuggleworthy bosom.'

She went scarlet—he seemed to enjoy her blush. She had thought him more or less out for the count when she had cradled him to her semi-naked breasts last night.

What was a girl to do? Emmie did the only thing possible. Regardless that he was her boss, she ordered, 'Clear off, Cunningham!' To her surprise, he went.

Emmie heard him moving around, but, though she wanted to leave her bed, she stayed where she was until she eventually heard him letting himself out of the flat. She got up then—and found she had wandered into the next-door room. He had made the bed he had slept in, she noted, and she fell in love with him all over again.

Aunt Hannah was in a talkative mood when Emmie went to collect her, telling her all about last night's play, and did Emmie mind if she didn't come next Saturday either; they were having a whist drive at Keswick House in the afternoon and it might go on until rather late.

In all the years Emmie had known her she had never known Aunt Hannah was interested in cards, much less a game of whist. But Emmie couldn't help but be pleased that—given a lapse here and there—the dear love seemed to be really, really settling in and treating Keswick House as her home.

Aunt Hannah had a nap after lunch, and Emmie picked up the paper to read. But she did not read very much. Barden was in her head again, dominating her thoughts. He'd looked so ill last night, barely able to stand. Of course he'd been well again this morning and—remembering that comment about her 'snuggleworthy bosom'—full of dev-ilment.

She found she was grinning, and straightened her face behind her newspaper. Then, recalling how a week tomorrow Barden was going to fly to the States for two weeks, she did not have to make a conscious effort to stop smiling. There wasn't a smile about her as she wondered how she was going to cope for *two whole weeks* without seeing him!

It had been bad enough on Friday, when she had believed she wouldn't see him again for two days. But two weeks! Why couldn't he have asked her to go with him? He could take a PA to Stratford; why couldn't he take a PA to the States?

She went to work on Monday knowing she couldn't have gone away—she had to be there for Aunt Hannah. To her delight, Emmie found Barden in good spirits. 'How's the fair Emily this morning?' he enquired, when she took some paperwork in to him.

Fair-complexioned but with black hair! She loved him. 'Very well,' she answered sedately, but just had to ask, 'Yourself?'

'Never had nursing like it,' he murmured, his expression dead-pan.

Emmie went a trifle pink and returned to her office, fairly certain Barden had been referring to her 'snuggleworthy bosom'.

He was in the same amiable mood the next day too, and, while he made no mention or hint again of having been in need on Saturday of what nursing skills she had, she had never known him so friendly and pleasant. All in all, she found him pretty wonderful.

So wonderful, so much in her head, that, had she not bumped into Simon Elsworth in one of the corridors, Emmie had an idea she'd have forgotten she had a date with him later that evening.

It was not a good evening. Simon Elsworth was a snob.

It showed in his face when he called for her, looking down his nose at the area where she had her flat. 'I'm glad you're ready,' he greeted her when she answered the door, 'I wouldn't want to leave my car unattended around here for more than a minute.'

Guess who wasn't going to be invited in for coffee at the end of the evening! 'Very wise,' she replied, and her love for Barden soared—he'd left his extremely expensive car outside for hours on end—all night once, only recently—and had never looked down at where she lived.

Because her heart wasn't in it, and that wasn't fair to her escort, Emmie put herself out to be a pleasing companion. She realised she'd succeeded when her enquiries caused Simon to talk expansively about himself.

'Would you like to come back to my place?' he asked at the end of the evening.

No mention of coffee! This is where I bale out! 'It's been a super evening.' Emmie smiled, and having learned that Simon Elsworth was very career-orientated, added, 'but it's rather late, and we both have to give of our best tomorrow.'

He tried to kiss her when they parted. She found the idea appalling! She'd hit him if he did. 'Goodnight,' she said firmly, pushing him away.

'Shall I see you again?'

Not if I see you first. 'You will,' she managed. 'Probably tomorrow, at work. Goodnight.' She went in. If he had anything to add she wasn't staying around to hear it.

Simon Elsworth had been a mistake, she mused as she went to work the next day. She had thought him shy and perhaps a little sensitive when she'd agreed to go out with him. She had been wrong. She recalled how he had attempted to kiss her last night—and her appalled reaction. Had falling in love with Barden spoiled her for other men? She rather thought so.

The day started well. Dawn seemed to be having a better time of it now, in the latter stage of her pregnancy. She seemed, too, to feel more and more confident about passing work over to her assistant.

So it was that Dawn left it mainly to her to deal with the paperwork their employer would be wanting on his American trip. Emmie still didn't know how she was going to cope with not seeing him for two weeks—sixteen days if you counted the Saturday and Sunday prior.

She decided to live for the moment and, breezing in cheerfully to Barden's office, saw him look up as she entered, his glance on her alive face. She went all weak and pathetic inside at just seeing him, and, knowing she'd be with him for some time, was glad to be able to turn away and close the door, taking the opportunity to pull herself together.

'The figures on…' she began as she turned back and took a seat—only to find that, for the moment, Barden had no interest in the information she had for him.

'Your love-life hasn't suffered, I trust?' he enquired affably.

Emmie did a massive switch to get on to his wavelength and realised he was referring to the fact that, having opened the door to Adrian early on Sunday morning trouserless, with only a robe for modesty, Adrian must know he'd stayed the night. 'Can't say that it has,' she replied calmly.

'He's forgiven you—Adrian?' Barden asked sharply.

His tone annoyed her. 'I don't know what happened in your dream, but according to my memory he didn't have anything to forgive!'

'You've been out with him again since last Thursday?'

Thursday! She vaguely recalled telling Barden that she was meeting someone when they got back from Stratford— the rest of it would never go from her mind. Barden had kissed her, had…

'I'm trying to forget Thursday!' she said shortly.

And could have punched his head when he just wouldn't leave it alone. 'Him or me?' he grated.

Adrian had never figured. But these were dangerous waters—the very place for a red herring. 'Neither of you should get your hopes up,' she retorted loftily. 'I was out with Simon last night.'

Oh, dear—he was not a happy bunny! Barden positively glowered at her, and she knew then that he objected to her familiarity in telling him not to get his hopes up. She knew all too well that Barden hoped for nothing from her, but what was she supposed to do—sit there meekly and say nothing? To be that meek, she had discovered, was not in her nature. Besides, it was he who had started this personal discussion, not her. But apparently he was bored with the subject.

'Let me see your paperwork,' he ordered bossily—she'd have liked to have poked him in the eye with it!

Wednesday ended badly. Her employer was in a pig of a mood for the rest of the day. Even a call from his 'friend' Karla didn't seem to cheer him any, and Emmie went home of the view that if Barden Cunningham went to the States and never came back that would be fine by her.

The feeling didn't last. Within half an hour of reaching her flat, she wanted to be back with him whatever his mood.

Aunt Hannah rang her that night, and, again proving how independent and settled in her new environment she was becoming, asked if Emmie would mind if she didn't come to lunch on Sunday.

'You're going somewhere nice?' Emmie asked, knowing she would miss her while at the same time being glad for her.

'We're having a residents' meeting to discuss what we can do for a charity fayre. Everyone does so much for us,' Aunt Hannah explained, 'we thought we'd like to pay something back. They'll take a bit of organising, of course,' she said, of her fellow residents, obviously one of the leaders, 'but everyone seems to be keen.'

'Let me know if I can help,' Emmie offered, and had to

smile when Aunt Hannah declared stoutly that she would, and meant it.

To Emmie's delight Barden seemed to have recovered his good humour the next day, and was back to being friendly, and, as far as Emmie was concerned, at his most endearing.

She heartily hoped he was the same when the following morning, while Dawn was in with him, Lisa Browne rang to say that Mrs Whitford had left without saying where she was going and had been away some while.

Emmie had just put the phone down when the connecting door opened and, standing back to allow Dawn to precede him, Barden came into her office.

Barden's glance went straight to Emmie. 'Problem, Emmie?' he enquired calmly, observing her anxious expression.

'Aunt Hannah, she's…'

'Decamped?' he finished for her. Emmie nodded. 'You've got your car?' he questioned.

'Yes.'

'Off you go, then,' he instructed kindly.

'I'm sorry,' she apologised, feeling suddenly wretched.

'Don't be—you'll be here until eight tonight.'

He smiled, she found a smile, and Dawn, who by then knew all about Aunt Hannah and her penchant for tripping the light fantastic, smiled warmly too—and Emmie wasted no more time.

She eventually found her absconding step-relative back at her flat, having let herself in. 'I thought, as I wouldn't be seeing you this weekend, that I'd come and see you today,' she announced, appearing totally oblivious that Emmie had a job to go to. 'Been shopping?' she enquired.

Emmie phoned Keswick House, then made some coffee and chatted, and at last was able to drive her much loved step-grandmother back to Keswick House. Emmie returned to her place of work to find that Dawn—who would be back later—had already left for her medical appointment, and that Barden, this being his last day in the office before his trip on Monday, was extremely busy.

He had time to ask if everything was all right, though, and Emmie was pleased to be able to tell him she had found Aunt Hannah at her flat. 'Which has to be a good sign,' she added. 'While it's a bit worrying that the rebel in her lets herself out of Keswick House without writing down where she's going in the "Out" book, it's good that she's remembered where I now live.'

She went back to her office and got on with some work, and was busily trying to make up for time lost when Barden strolled into her office. She looked up, expecting instruction of some sort, while trying to pretend that the next sixteen days without seeing him weren't going to be as bleak as she knew they were going to be.

But she was totally staggered when what Barden had come to see her about turned out to be nothing at all to do with work. He stated, 'I was very interested in some of the motorcycles on display the other Saturday.'

'The other Saturday when you were conned into taking Aunt Hannah to the Motorcycle Museum?' she asked, endeavouring her hardest to keep up.

'I wouldn't have put it exactly like that myself,' he murmured charmingly. 'I wonder, though, since I wouldn't mind going again tomorrow, if Mrs Whitford would like to come with me?'

'You want to take Aunt Hannah to Birmingham, to the...' Emmie stared at him, open-mouthed.

'We'll let you come with us if you promise to behave yourself,' he offered casually—and her heart sang, her spirits soared. If she saw him again tomorrow, that would make it only fifteen days.

Then her spirits sank. She could have wept. It wasn't fair. She loved him, and it just wasn't fair. 'Normally Aunt Hannah would have loved it.' She smiled—that or cry, and a girl did have some pride. 'But I'm not seeing her this weekend. That's part of the reason she came to see me today—she forgot I go to work.' Oh, crumbs, he wasn't interested in that; pull yourself together, do. 'I'm sorry.' Emmie rose above her crushing disappointment, 'I really appreciate your kindness, but Aunt Hannah has other plans for Saturday and Sunday, and I won't see her at all this weekend.'

'It was just a thought,' he said, and with that he returned to his office and, while feeling like howling, Emmie pretended to be never happier. But her feeling of utter wretchedness was compounded by a giant-size green blip when Karla Nesbitt rang to speak to Barden. Emmie put her through and knew that motorcycle museums would be the last thing on his mind for tomorrow.

Dawn left at five, but Emmie stayed on working with Barden until, just after seven, she took in the last of her paperwork and prepared to go home. 'That's everything,' she confirmed. 'I hope you have a good trip.' Take me with you, oh, please take me with you. 'I'll see you when you get back,' she chirruped lightly, and he'd never know how leaden her heart felt.

Barden was on his feet, his expression solemn, 'Be good, Emily Lawson,' he bade her.

'You too,' she smiled, and turned quickly away so he shouldn't see how her smile was slipping. She went home.

Emmie had seen Adrian briefly a couple of times in the week, and had been grateful that if he was curious about her ill-fitting-robe-clad overnight visitor he'd held his curiosity down. He dropped in for a coffee on Saturday morning, and was again unprying. But it was a sad fact that seeing Adrian was about the biggest highlight of that miserable Saturday for Emmie. She was certain that Barden was out with Karla Nesbitt.

She got out of bed on Sunday determined to keep busy,

but her flat was clean and shining from her efforts yesterday, and what chores she could find were soon completed.

Feeling unbearably restless, she took herself off for a walk—Barden was with her every step of the way. She found it was no use telling herself no good could come of her love for Barden; she already knew that. But it didn't make her feelings for him go away.

She returned to her flat, resolved her love for him was not going to make the slightest difference to her, and cooked a meal which she couldn't eat. Which was ridiculous. Womanising swine. She'd bet he never lost his appetite. He was probably tucking into his lunch right this minute—most likely with Karla Nesbitt as his companion. Emmie felt sick at heart when her mind ballooned to what else he might have an appetite for.

It was later that day, when the time had dragged around to just after six, when the phone rang in her silent flat, and Emmie nearly jumped out of her skin. She went to answer it.

'Hello?' she said, and nearly jumped again when she heard Barden's voice.

'You're not with anyone, I trust?' he enquired.

Like who? Pride arrived and shored up her melting bones. What about him? Was Karla with him? Oh, clear off, jealousy, you're making me ill. 'Why?' she asked, not about to let him know there wasn't a man about the place.

'I wondered if you could possibly come over and take some notes.'

Notes! They'd completed all his work Friday! Or so she'd thought. Perhaps, though, he'd spent the afternoon in his study and... The sun suddenly came out. His only appetite was—for work?

'Can't I take notes over the phone?' Instantly she wanted the words back. Clown! She'd just die if he said yes, and she lost this precious chance to see him again before he flew off.

'I'll give you dinner,' he coaxed, and Emmie loved him so much that, on hearing that friendly coaxing note, she felt she would do anything he asked.

'You're cooking it?' She couldn't keep a smile out of her voice.

'My housekeeper,' he replied.

She knew his home was called Hazeldene and was about an hour's run away. 'You'd better give me some directions,' she agreed, and delayed only long enough after his call to take a rapid shower, apply a little make-up and do a hasty check of her wardrobe.

Her red dress of fine wool won. She knew it suited her. It had short sleeves, a round neck and was perfectly plain. Emmie surveyed her reflection prior to donning her coat; her night-black hair was shiny and she had an excited light in her eyes. She'd have to watch that. But—she couldn't wait any longer. And, all right, so it was work, but—Barden was waiting to see her.

Her heart raced all the time while, following his directions, she drove nearer to his home. It seemed to race even faster when she turned into the driveway of Hazeldene, a large Georgian residence in its own grounds.

Leaving her car, she crossed the gravelled drive to the stout front door and rang the bell, but was not left waiting long before it was answered. She had supposed it would be his housekeeper who might open the door. But, and before Emmie was ready, it was Barden himself who stood there.

Swiftly she lowered her eyes—oh, how she loved him. 'Oh, hello,' she offered casually. 'Your housekeeper's busy in the kitchen?' she followed up, wanting to die at the inanity of her remark, feeling it was going to rank as one of those idiotic comments that come back again and again to haunt you.

'Dinner's all prepared—I've given Mrs Trevor the rest of the evening off,' Barden replied easily. If he thought her comment idiotic, he wasn't showing it for a moment.

'Come in, Emmie. I was beginning to think my directions were at fault.'

Emmie crossed the threshold into a wide and thickly carpeted hall, a smile playing around her mouth when, thinking she might have got there a trifle too quickly, it seemed Barden had expected her sooner.

'Let me have your coat,' he suggested, guiding her further along the hall and opening one of the many doors to reveal a downstairs cloakroom. Emmie shrugged out of her coat and he took it from her and hung it up, his eyes flicking over her and her red dress as he turned back to her. 'You've never worn that to the office,' he commented briefly.

'You'd have remembered?' She hadn't meant to be provocative—the words had just slipped out. 'I m-mean,' she stammered, 'I don't remember every suit you wear.'

'But then I never look anywhere as noteworthy as you,' he answered, his mouth curving slightly upwards at the corners.

She was in a meltdown situation again. He thought her noteworthy! She fought valiantly against his least little pleasantry affecting her, and managed some semblance of a brain cell by uttering, 'Talking of notes, I forgot to bring a notepad.'

'Not an insurmountable problem—I hardly expected you to.' He smiled, charmed her to her marrow, and, touching her lightly on her elbow, he led the way across the hall to a small kind of ante-room that housed an over-large thickly padded deep-cushioned sofa, an equally over-large thickly padded and deep-cushioned chair, and a couple of tables, one of which was close up to the sofa and carried a telephone and a sheaf of paperwork. 'I thought we'd work in here,' he informed her. 'A bit more congenial for a Sunday than my study.'

He made it seem more personal than business, and

Emmie was delighted. 'Anything you say,' she answered agreeably.

'According to Mrs Trevor, I'm to do things domestic in half an hour.'

'Has she written it down?' Emmie heard herself tease. Oh, Lord—get a grip!

Barden's mouth twitched. 'For that, you can have the burned bit,' he threatened, and she loved him. Then he said, 'We'll sit over there and I can give you an outline before we eat, then you can ask any questions during our meal.'

'Fine,' she answered, 'over there' being the over-large sofa. She went over to it and tried to calm the wild drumming of her heart when Barden, taking up the sheaf of paperwork, came and sat beside her.

'This is a list of…' he began, and Emmie realised why he was sitting that bit nearer to her when he extended the paper he had in his hand so she should read it with him.

Donning her professional hat, she moved in closer, raising a hand to the paper to get the view she wanted. Unfortunately her fingers touched his, and a kind of tingly sensation shot through her. She jerked back—and bumped against Barden.

And he, as she knew, never missed a thing. He turned in his seat to look at her. 'You're—twitchy,' he accused, his tone gentle, surprised even.

He was too close; his body, his face were too close. 'No, I'm not,' she denied, but for all she was trying desperately to stay professional her voice came out sounding all husky, and every bit as though she felt far from relaxed.

Barden's expression softened, and tenderly almost he trailed the back of his left hand down the side of her face. 'I'm sorry, Emmie,' he said kindly, 'perhaps working in here wasn't such a very good idea after all.'

'Are you deliberately trying to embarrass me?' she demanded, waking up with a vengeance—good grief, he was as good as saying that he was aware he had some kind of effect on her, over and above their employer-employee relationship.

'What a sensitive soul you are!' Barden's tone was still kindly. 'Of course I'm not trying to embarrass you. Though I have to say that I'm—aware,' he selected, as if choosing his words carefully, 'of a chemistry between you and me that I'd prefer we kept under control.'

Talk about telling the truth and shaming the devil! She felt red up to the top of her ears. 'Speak for yourself, Mr Cunningham,' she stated bluntly. 'In the past you have kissed me; I don't recall that I reciprocated in any way!' She was ready to go home. To blazes with his notes!

What she wasn't ready for was that Barden should look at her, slightly amazed, and then give a short bark of laughter. 'A gentleman might let that pass, but…'

'But you're no gentleman,' she finished for him, having to cast her mind back to only a week last Thursday to recall how he had kissed her and how she had put her arms around him and had wanted more of his kisses.

'You'd prefer I lied—let you lie?'

'I prefer nothing—I'm going home!' she snapped, and hated him and his wretched over-cushioned sofa because, when she went to struggle out of its depths, it seemed determined to hang on to her.

Needing a bit of leverage, she pressed her hands down, one to the sofa at one side of her, the other down somehow on him—his well-muscled thigh. As though scalded she snatched her hand away, and Barden stretched out a hand to steady her—and somehow they ended up being closer than ever.

'Don't let's part bad friends,' he said softly—and her backbone went liquid again.

'Barden…' she murmured helplessly. The only thing in her head then was that he was going away tomorrow for two weeks, for two whole miserable, agonising tortoise-ticking weeks, and she didn't want to part bad friends.

'Shall we kiss and make up?' he teased gently. It was the best suggestion she'd heard in a long while.

'As long as you don't accuse me of over-reciprocating,' she laughed—and reciprocated fully at the first touch of his mouth against her own.

He was going away. Two endlessly long weeks would pass before she saw him again was all she could think of as Barden gathered her into his arms. And, when one kiss just wasn't enough, she was enraptured by their mutual reciprocation.

'I shall miss you while I'm away,' he said against her mouth—and it was the nicest thing anyone had ever said to her. She wanted to tell him that she would miss him too, but she was shy, and then the moment was past, because his lips claimed hers once more and she couldn't have spoken had she been able to overcome that shyness.

'Barden.' She said his name breathlessly as that kiss ended.

'Emmie,' he murmured, just that, and nothing more. Nothing more was needed as his head came near again and he looked deeply into her warm and giving velvety brown eyes.

He kissed her then, gently at first before, his kiss gaining in intensity at her response, he held her yet closer to him and touched her lips with his tongue. While she clutched at him and her lips parted so passion flared again, soared, and Emmie was then mindless of all and everything save him and how he made her feel.

She wanted him, wanted him with everything that was in her. Mutually they seemed to lie down together, wrapped together in the cushions of the sofa. She felt the hard length of him as body to body, thigh to thigh they pressed against each other.

With a gentle, unhurried touch, Barden caressed her, and when his hands moved to the fastening of her dress Emmie felt not the slightest alarm. She kissed him as, without haste, he took her dress from her, excitement drumming in her temples. She unbuttoned his shirt, vaguely aware he had been wearing a light sweater when she'd arrived but having no notion as to when he had disposed of it.

'You're beautiful, Emmie, so beautiful,' he breathed, staring down at her. She smiled, an all-giving smile, and he lowered his head, and thrilled her with more kisses, a hand whisperingly caressing her right shoulder, to gradually move her bra strap to one side.

Barden kissed the satin-smooth skin of her shoulder, and trailed his mouth down to her breast. She felt a surge of shyness again when he caressed her breast and then undid her bra fastening.

'Barden!' she exclaimed huskily.

'Is that a "don't"?' he said softly.

She melted again. 'I think—I'm not so used to this,' she said on a little gulp of breath.

'I know,' he answered understandingly.

'Oh, Barden,' she sighed, and, every movement unhurried, he gently removed her bra.

'May I look?' he requested, a teasing kind of note there, for all—or maybe because—he must know she had never been this intimate with a man before.

She almost told him then that she loved him. But swallowed once more instead, and asked, 'May I look at you?' and loved him some more when he understood that too, because he removed his shirt, and Emmie, in a kind of awe, stared at his broad manly chest—naked except for a liberal sprinkling of darkish hair. 'Oh,' she said, and liked as well as loved it when he didn't ask what the 'oh' was about.

Instead, he lowered his gaze to her entirely uncovered breasts. 'Oh, Emmie,' he murmured. 'Emmie, sweetheart.' And while she thrilled at his endearment he bent and kissed her lips, and she felt the warmth of his naked chest against her naked skin.

She had an idea she sighed his name again, but she

couldn't be sure about anything any more because while he kissed her, Barden's hands were caressing and stroking the swollen globes of her breasts, and desire for him was rising and rising in her. She wanted him; more than anything she wanted him. She loved him and wanted him.

He lowered his head to her breasts, nibbled at the hardened pink tip and must have known as she clutched at his naked back that he was making her mindless with wanting.

They lay close again, and as their legs entwined she suddenly realised—strangely without panic—that while she had been unaware of everything, save him and the riot of emotions he was evoking in her, he had parted with his trousers. Then was when she experienced a few moments of panic. But then, too, she experienced a person she had never known she could be—an aroused woman who delighted in stroking his hair-roughened chest, who delighted in touching him. Instinctively she stretched, to nibble and kiss his manly nipples, and heard a groan of wanting leave him. She felt his hands on her behind—if she'd been wearing tights, and she had been, she had no idea where they were now.

The intimacy of the warmth of his hands as they caressed inside her briefs made her clutch on to him, and she heard a sound of joyous delight as he pulled her to lie over him, just as if he was saying, At your pace, Emmie, at your pace. Again, as she lay over him, their legs entwined; she kissed him.

From far off she heard the sound of a telephone ringing, but it had nothing to do with her and Barden. She kissed him, touched her tongue to his lips the way his had touched hers. The phone continued to ring. She halted.

'Ignore it—and do that again,' Barden commanded.

Emmie was happy to oblige. She pressed herself to him, kissing him—and heard a groan that was most definitely the sound, even to her novice ears, of a man desirous of making complete love to her. His hands under her remaining garment pulled her yet closer to him, and—had it not been for the unremitting ring of the unanswered phone—Emmie would have been utterly captivated, utterly his for the taking.

But that phone, nearer at hand than she'd realised when she raised her head, was an unwanted intrusion in this new and enchanted land.

Emmie stretched out a hand to the offending instrument with no idea if she meant to merely stop it ringing or whether, perhaps from habit, to route the caller to Barden so that he, in the fewest words possible, should end the intrusion. Her mind, she had to admit, was totally elsewhere when, receiver in hand, she raised it in passing against her ear.

Only—she didn't get to proceed with the manoeuvre. Not then. For, chortling across the airwaves, she distinctly heard an all-male voice order in jocular fashion, 'Stop seducing your secretary, Barden, and speak to me!' And shock waves immediately swamped her.

As if someone had just thrown a bucket of icy water over her, Emmie came rocketing to her senses. Though not much was making sense to her just then—other than the appalling truth. Barden must have been in this situation many times before! Barden, to the caller's certain knowledge, was no stranger to the seduction couch! Barden—Barden the womaniser—had *planned* this seduction, *her* seduction! But she, she meant nothing to him!

Horrified, sick at heart at his treachery, she threw the phone at him and grabbed for her clothes. 'What...?' he began, moving to sit up as she leapt from the sofa. But she was off—if he had anything else to add, Emmie was in no mood to hear it.

CHAPTER SEVEN

AT LEAST if Emmie had had her way she would have shot out of Barden's home without saying another word to him. But there was the small matter of getting dressed and collecting her coat from the cloakroom first, and she hadn't so much as got the zip of her dress done up before she heard him tell his caller, 'I'll ring you,' and, that dealt with, Barden was off the sofa and trying to take a hold of her right arm.

'Don't touch me!' she yelled, backing, fumbling with her zip, her agitation wild. 'And put some clothes on!' she snapped—what she didn't need was to see him so deliciously near naked; her wayward senses were still threatening to make a nonsense of her.

To her surprise, though she was sure that it wasn't in order to calm her, Barden complied. By the time she was properly zipped up and attired—and making for the door—he was once more trouser- and shirt-clad, and having the effrontery to try to detain her.

'Don't go!' He attempted to halt her at the door.

'Would you mind getting out of my way?' Emmie demanded icily. She had to go; she was barely thinking straight—and she *needed* to think.

'You're in no state to drive,' he declared, refusing to allow her to open the door. 'Stay...'

'Like hell!' she breathed, and with power she hadn't known she possessed she wrenched the door open and sprinted across the hall to the cloakroom.

She had the cloakroom door open, and was reaching for her coat, when Barden's hand on her wrist stopped her.

140

'You're scared,' he gentled, his tone soothing. 'I've frightened you. I'm sorry, but I wouldn't…'

She snatched her wrist out of his grasp—he was just *too* much. 'You're darned right you wouldn't!' she yelled, still fearing that if he didn't let go she might yet give in to him. 'I wouldn't let you!' she stormed, and, her coat in her hand, she went flying to the door, yanking it open—only to be stunned by the sight of a most ravishing blonde who was just about to ring the doorbell.

'Karla!' Barden exclaimed, and Emmie didn't wait to hear any more.

Without a please or thank you, she pushed past Karla Nesbitt, hating her, hating him, and hoping to make it to her car before she broke down.

Emmie was in her car and had it moving, realising she had reserves of strength she'd never known about, because she wasn't yet in floods of tears. Someone banged on the driver's window.

She jerkily glanced up to see Barden, in his shirtsleeves on a freezing night, standing there clearly demanding she opened her window. She did—just sufficiently so he should hear. 'Do me a favour—catch pneumonia!' Then she put her foot down.

She saw him in her rearview mirror, just standing there. The next time she looked he'd gone. Five minutes later, though, and she saw there was a car following her. She had to slow down at some traffic lights—it was Barden's car. Obviously the cold night hadn't cooled his ardour!

Emmie jetted away from the lights and drove speedily and erratically and, she had to admit, just a little crazily for the next five or so miles. She had been paying pretty constant attention to her rearview mirror, but the next time she looked, there was no other car in sight.

Nor, as she proceeded the rest of the way more soberly, did Barden appear behind her again. No doubt he'd gone back to the waiting Karla, Emmie fumed, thoughts rattling around in her head about the way Barden had set the scene—even to the extent of giving his housekeeper the night off! And how more than likely, at this very moment, Karla Nesbitt would have taken her place on that well-padded deeply cushioned sofa.

By the time Emmie reached her flat she had convinced herself that Barden Cunningham was 'celebrating' his departure for the States tomorrow with someone else—namely Karla.

Emmie had only just got in when her phone started to ring. It wouldn't be him? Would it? Don't be stupid; he was busy finding his way around Karla's zippers and fasteners. Oh, how she hated him.

Her phone continued to ring—she determined not to answer it. That was until conscience-twisting thoughts that it might be Aunt Hannah phoning for a chat started to plague her.

She'd answer it—but she wasn't going to speak to *him*—if him it was. Emmie picked up the phone and said not a word—neither did the party at the other end. Which told her that it wasn't Aunt Hannah—it was unknown for her aunt to hold back.

The silence grew, persisted—Emmie broke first. 'And you can stuff your dinner!' she yelled. Silently, her caller terminated the call. A swift dialling of 1471 revealed that the caller's number was not known.

She knew then that it hadn't been Aunt Hannah, and, glad to feel hate for Barden Cunningham, Emmie went and got ready for bed. Then discovered that it was pointless having an early night—her head was too busy for sleep.

So much for that loathsome rat saying he'd prefer to keep the chemistry between them under control! All he'd been doing had been lulling her into a false sense of security—she could see that now. No wonder he'd given his housekeeper the rest of the night off. He wouldn't want his Mrs

Trevor bursting into that small and—what was it?—'more congenial for a Sunday' ante-room, would he? I'll say it was congenial. Just nice and cosy for a 'congenial' seduction.

Which brought her straight back to the stunning-looking Karla Nesbitt. Oh, how she wished she had never laid eyes on her. It had been enough to know of Karla's existence— to see for sure, as anticipated, that Karla was elegant and sophisticated into the bargain, was something Emmie just hadn't needed. What Karla was doing ringing the doorbell at Hazeldene Emmie had no wish to speculate. But—didn't seem able to stop herself from doing so. Had Barden thought her 'note-taking' wouldn't take all that long? Had he arranged for Karla to call later? Hang on, though, even as fresh spiteful jealous barbs speared her Emmie was recalling that Barden had definitely mentioned dinner. He'd definitely invited her to dinner. So where did Karla come in? Perhaps for the sweet course, Emmie thought sourly.

Endeavouring to get both Barden Cunningham and Karla Nesbitt out of her head, Emmie was forced to come to the sad conclusion that if Barden had *not* been expecting Karla to call—and from the way Emmie remembered it Karla hadn't been on his mind at the time—then the blonde sophisticate must be on *very* friendly terms with him. Who but a very good female friend would just drop by without thinking to make a prior arrangement? He had, Emmie recalled—remembering his exclaimed 'Karla!' when he'd seen her—been a shade surprised to see her on his doorstep.

After a fitful night with Barden, and a liberal sprinkling of Karla, filling her head, Emmie got up at her usual time the next morning, but had never felt less like going to work. She got ready just the same, and was within ten minutes of leaving her flat when her phone rang. She knew it wouldn't be Barden this time—by her reckoning he was on his way to the airport.

'Hello?' she queried, on lifting the receiver—and nearly dropped it when Barden answered.

'I hoped I'd get you before you left for the office,' he informed her, sounding cool and in charge and just the same as he always did—and, while she had spent the most wretched of nights, it was all too plain that he hadn't missed a wink of sleep.

It just wasn't fair! Her pride came rushing to the fore, refusing to be stamped down when all logic would have advised caution. 'I'm not going to the office,' she told him loftily—put that in your flute and play it!

'You're not?'

Oh, dear, there was a definite edge coming to his voice. 'Not!' She refused to back down—and pride pushed her on. 'I'm leaving,' announced pride, when its owner knew she just couldn't afford to give up this job that paid so well.

But she had angered him, she realised, either by her words or the lofty way she'd said them. Before she could retract her statement that she intended leaving he, to her absolute dismay, was snarling furiously, 'Correction, Miss Lawson—you've left!'

'Left!' she gasped witlessly. 'How…?' She started to get herself together. 'You're dismissing me?' she challenged— her own anger not very far behind his. 'On what grounds?' she demanded. If he so much as mentioned their 'chemistry' last night, she'd…

'Try misinformation at job interview!' He stopped her dead in her tracks.

'You *pig*! You utter pig! You know…'

'I know that you were lying your pretty little head off at your job interview when you were misinforming me about your lack of commitments. I've since learned for myself of your tardiness with regard to time-keeping, I—'

'I was late *once*!' she butted in stormily.

'Not to mention your absenteeism,' he went on, as though he hadn't heard her.

'I've always made that lost time up!' she flared angrily.

Only to have her pride rear up totally out of her control when, his anger dipping slightly, he mockingly drawled, 'Anyone would think you didn't want to leave after all, Emily.'

And that taunt was just too much. 'You can keep your job, Cunningham!'' she yelled. 'I wouldn't work for you if you paid me triple and in diamonds!' It was a toss-up which one of them ended the call first.

For all of five minutes after the call ended Emmie fumed about her ex-employer. The reality started to descend. Oh, pride, wretched, wretched pride—I just can't afford you, Emmie realised.

Where Dawn was concerned there were several people who sprang to mind who would be more than willing to help her out, Emmie knew. Which didn't make Emmie feel any less guilty for not being there to help the mother-to-be. From her own point of view, though, she needed that job—oh, what an idiot, love, pride and all else had made her.

Although, thinking about it, she had to be glad she had acted the way she had. Because, on playing back her conversation with Barden, as she did many times in the next hour, Emmie came to realise that, starting with 'I hoped I'd get you before you left for the office' Barden had only been ringing anyway to tell her not to go to the office—ever again.

She was glad, glad, glad she'd got in first to tell him she was leaving. Which was not at all conducive to her earning her living. She toyed with the idea of ringing Dawn and apologising for leaving so abruptly, but guessed that Mr Efficiency would have been in touch—either before or after his call to her—acquainting Dawn with the news. And anyhow, Dawn might well ask awkward questions, such as why, if Barden hadn't told Dawn why he'd sacked her, she had left. She could hardly tell Dawn that Barden had been in the middle of seducing her when, almost too late, she'd come to her senses.

Instead of ringing Dawn, Emmie rang a temping agency, went for interview, and found work to keep her busy to the end of that week. She rang Lisa Browne at Keswick House to tell her where she could be contacted, and found the temporary work uncomplicated and unchallenging. She bought a paper on her way home to check the 'Situations Vacant' column.

There was nothing remotely as good as the job she had that very morning been dismissed from. Emmie determined she would not be down-hearted. She invited Adrian for a meal the next night, and heard he had bumped into his ex-girlfriend and had her new phone number—and was hopeful.

Emmie wished him well, it was a little cheering to hear of someone else's love-life taking a bit of an upward swing—hers was at rock-bottom, as were her spirits. There were no Situations Vacant that sounded in the least appealing that night either.

Determined to look on the bright side, she rang Aunt Hannah after her meal on Wednesday evening. 'You've nothing planned for this weekend, I hope?' she managed to tease.

'I'll come to you Saturday afternoon, if I may—I'll be glad of a break. We've got a meeting here on Saturday morning, but trying to get this lot here to agree to anything is impossible—they're worse than a lot of schoolchildren.'

For all her step-relative was having a general moan, she sounded in a happy frame of mind, and positive about having been elected to be part of the recently formed residents' committee.

Emmie came away from the phone resolving to be more positive herself. To that end she circled three possibles in that evening's Situations Vacant column, and took out her writing materials.

She had penned only one application, however, when her phone rang. She wasn't expecting a call, and had just spoken with Aunt Hannah. But it was not unknown for Aunt Hannah to ring back with something she had forgotten. Emmie answered the phone with a warm and pleasant, 'Hello?'

She immediately went from warm and pleasant to shocked and stunned when her call turned out to be of the transatlantic variety. 'Hello, Emmie,' Barden greeted her, his tone a shade on the cool side, she rather thought, but hadn't got her head sufficiently together to be very sure about that. But, whatever his tone, hers was non-existent when her voice failed her completely. 'It occurred to me,' he went on, when nothing at all came from her, 'that perhaps we were both a little over-hasty the last time I rang.'

Her heart was racing. What was he saying? She tried desperately to fight against the love-weakened shell she had become, who wanted to agree with everything he said. 'You may have been—I wasn't!' she found out of a stubborn somewhere. Was he saying that she wasn't dismissed after all? Her brain started to stir—she wanted to work for him, she did, she did, but...

'Oh, come on, Emmie, you know you need to work,' Barden said toughly—and Emmie woke up with a bang.

He was *pitying* her! How *dared* he? He knew her financial situation, the fact that she needed the kind of salary he paid but—how dared he pity her? She wanted his love, not his pity.

'I *am* working!' she snapped, proud and starting to be furious into the bargain.

'*Where?*'

It hadn't taken long for his aggression to arrive on the scene, had it! 'That's none of your business!' she retorted hotly. 'I shan't be asking you for a reference!' With that, afraid her tongue might run away with her, and that she might reveal some of her hurt, Emmie slammed down her phone.

It did not ring again that night, and Emmie spent the rest of the evening—her letters of application forgotten—in knowing she had done the only thing possible. But that didn't make her feel any better.

Logic, screaming logic, stabbed at her the whole of the time, reminding her—as if she needed any reminding—that she just couldn't afford to turn down the chance of reinstatement in a job that paid so well.

But, ignoring logic, her emotions well and truly out of gear, she had turned down that chance. She wished Barden had not telephoned, and yet—and she owned that love had made her a mass of contradictions—she hungered for the sound of his voice.

But she couldn't take his pity. No way did she *want* his pity. She had seen his kindness before, and guessed that his motive in calling her had probably stemmed from that quality she had witnessed in him.

For ageless minutes Emmie dwelt on his goodness of heart—only to come to minutes later to recall the enchantment of being in his arms on Sunday, and to start to discount entirely that his motives had been kindness at all.

The miserable toad had set her up last Sunday—don't forget that, Emily Lawson. For heaven's sake, was she so naive that she couldn't see further than the end of her nose? Seduction was the name of the game here, not kindness.

Well, forget it, Mr Won't-take-no-for-an-answer Cunningham. She was not going to be 'one of his women'. Just as she was not going back to work for him. Neither was she going to have an affair with him—the ultimate outcome of which would only mean job loss anyway—and Aunt Hannah's security was still, as it had to be, of prime importance.

Emmie sighed—perhaps she'd got it wrong and he didn't want an affair. But what did she know? What she *did* know was that she loved him so, and that from the way their telephone conversation had ended she reckoned there was a good chance that an affair was off the menu. She went to bed with a throbbing head.

The weekend arrived on leaden feet, and on Saturday morning, after a few chores, Emmie took herself off bright and early to the shops. She would be picking up Aunt Hannah that afternoon—Aunt Hannah, different to the last, preferred 'shop' cake to home-made. Emmie was quite laden by the time she got back.

She was just about to go up the steps to the house when Adrian came bounding out—she had never seen him looking so happy! 'I saw you from my window!' he announced, smiling broadly.

'You've passed all your exams!' she teased.

'Is it obvious?' he asked, automatically taking some of her plastic carriers. 'Better than that—' he grinned joyously '—I've just rung Tina—she's agreed to go out with me tonight!'

They were standing at the bottom of the steps and, had her hands not been full, Emmie felt so pleased for him she might have given him a hug. She settled for giving him a beaming smile—and discovered that Adrian was so ecstatic he could barely contain himself and, on impulse, leaned forward and kissed her.

He had never done such a thing before, but, while she was unoffended, he looked a little startled by his own behaviour. He was still on cloud nine, though, when he suggested, 'Fancy a cup of coffee?'

'I'd better make it,' she agreed. 'From the look of you, you'd probably end up scalding yourself.'

Adrian helped carry her shopping into her flat, but could talk of little else but Tina and his good fortune. 'She's not the sort of woman who would accept an invitation to go out with me if she was only playing,' he opined, and regaled Emmie with his hopes for the future and how he would take great care not to neglect Tina ever again if they ever did get back together again, as he so sincerely hoped.

He was still on a high, whistling his little head off, as she saw him out and he went up to his own flat. Emmie couldn't have been more pleased for him. But, with Barden ever a dominant force, Adrian was soon forgotten. It seemed to be a waste of effort trying to out Barden from her mind. Perhaps one day soon more than thirty seconds would tick by without him paying her head a visit.

She was never hungry these days, but forced herself to eat a snack before she left her flat just after two to go and pick up Aunt Hannah. The weather had improved, and while still cold it was sunny as Emmie parked her car and rang the bell at Keswick House.

A care assistant Emmie hadn't seen before answered the door to her. 'Mrs Whitford is expecting me,' Emmie began to explain.

'She's gone out,' June, according to her lapel badge, replied.

'Out?' Oh, crumbs—keep calm. She might have taken it into her head to come to her by taxi. 'Er—did Mrs Whitford say where she was going?' Emmie asked.

'She did,' June replied, and Emmie began to relax a little—at least Aunt Hannah hadn't done one of her little flits. 'She wrote the address down in the book,' the care assistant added, though she did pause to ask what her connection with Mrs Whitford was, and, when Emmie enlightened her, she invited her in.

'I expect Mrs Whitford has taken a taxi to see me.' Emmie smiled, wanting to be on her way and to get back home before Aunt Hannah should take it into her head to wander off. But, fully expecting that when June had inspected the 'Out' book she would say Aunt Hannah had filled in Emmie's address, Emmie got the shock of her life when June read an entirely different address from the book.

'She's gone to... Can't read her writing. Hazeldene. That's it. Is that where you live?'

'*Hazeldene!*' Emmie gasped.

'Yes, it's in...'

Emmie knew full well where Hazeldene was. 'Let me see,' she requested, more sharply than she'd meant to, hoping against hope that June had read it incorrectly—though since the house where she lived didn't have a name she feared the worst.

The care assistant, starting to look concerned, showed her the book—and there it was, Hazeldene, followed by most of the rest of Barden's address. 'There's nothing wrong, is there?' June asked. 'I mean, she told Mrs Vellacott she'd been invited to lunch and...'

To lunch! Ye gods! 'No, everything's fine,' Emmie assured her—and got out of there as quickly as she could.

She drove fast, trying not to panic. Invited to lunch? Where on earth had Aunt Hannah got that idea from? Emmie sped towards Hazeldene, trying to remember when she had ever told Aunt Hannah where her employer lived.

She couldn't actually remember ever having told her. That wasn't to say, though, that she never had, because she and Aunt Hannah discussed all sorts of inconsequential matters. And, of course, since Barden had been out for hours with Aunt Hannah that day he had taken her to the Motorcycle Museum, he could very likely have revealed to her himself where he lived.

With her mind in a turmoil Emmie slowed down as she turned into the drive at Hazeldene, her eyes scanning right and left and everywhere, hoping for a sight of Aunt Hannah. But of Aunt Hannah she saw not a sign.

Emmie parked her car and got out, her eyes still searching. She approached the stout front door and stood at the doorbell she had rung what seemed a lifetime away but was in fact only last Sunday. Perhaps the housekeeper would tell her if Aunt Hannah had called. Perhaps she could leave a message if she hadn't.

Emmie stretched a hand and rang the bell, hoping against hope that Mrs Trevor was in. Her only relief in any of this was that Barden, thank goodness, was absent in America, and with luck would never get to hear of any of it.

The stout front door began to open, and as her heart started to thunder so, with ever-widening astonished eyes, Emmie stared at the tall, no-nonsense grey-eyed man who stood there. Luck! Emmie knew then that her luck had just run out. What was Barden doing here? He was supposed to be on the other side of the Atlantic!

Without speaking, Barden, since it was she who had slammed the phone down on him the last time they had been in communication, politely waited for her to speak. For no reason—though half a dozen presented themselves, not least the one that the last time he had seen her she had been as near naked as made no difference—Emmie went scarlet.

'Is Aunt Hannah here?' came hurtling from her like a shot from a cannon.

Her question went unanswered—but he wasn't cutting her dead. 'Come in,' Barden invited, his eyes on her flushed skin, a smile lurking there somewhere.

Emmie had enough to cope with without her heart racing energetically to see him so unexpectedly. But she was grateful that he wasn't ordering her off his premises, and entered his home. She had thought he might ask while they were where they stood why she thought her step-relative might be paying him a visit, but he led the way into a superb drawing room that had several rather special-looking oil paintings adorning its walls, was thickly carpeted and housed several deeply cushioned sofas, similar to the one she had seen—experienced—in the ante-room.

She needed a clear head, and didn't want to think about the sofa experience, or any of it. 'Aunt Hannah…' she began rapidly. Only the rest of the sentence got lost somewhere when she saw Barden turn at the drawing room door and firmly close it.

He turned back to her. 'Take a seat, Emmie,' he invited, calm, where a riot of emotions were battering at *her*.

She declined. 'Aunt H—'

'Mrs Whitford is safe.' He put her mind at rest straight away.

'You've seen her? She's been here?' She was gabbling; Emmie slowed down. 'You say she's safe. Safe where?'

The smile that had been promising didn't make it. Seriously Barden studied her for long, silent moments before he at last revealed, 'Mrs Whitford's out with my father, actually.'

Emmie's wide eyes grew larger. 'Your—father?' she gasped, feeling a need to check on her hearing.

'He's taken her for a spin in his Austin Healey,' Barden stunned her further. 'She was delighted to go,' he added pleasantly.

Austin Healey! Delighted…! Of course she would be. She'd be tickled pink at the thought of having a drive in his father's classic car. Oh, heavens, this was so embarrassing. Obviously Barden's father had been paying him a visit when Aunt Hannah had arrived. Just as she'd conned Barden into taking her to Birmingham that time, she had probably seen the Austin Healey parked outside and had persuaded his father to take her for a drive in it.

'I'm sorry,' she mumbled miserably, loyalty to her step-relative preventing her from adding more of an apology than that. 'Um—have you any idea how long they'll be?'

Barden studied his watch. 'About an hour or so, I should think,' he answered, still in that same pleasant tone.

'Thank you,' Emmie said primly, making for the door and expecting him to move away from it. 'I'll come back later, if I may,' she stated politely.

Barden was already shaking his head, and had not moved

so much as a half-inch to let her out from the door. 'I don't think so,' he informed her coolly.

'You—don't think…' She halted. She was shaking inside already. *This* close was close enough. She got herself into more of one piece. 'Surely you can't object if I wait outside for my step-grandmother to return,' she challenged firmly—and was totally foxed for several seconds when it appeared that that was exactly what he did do.

'I object most strongly,' Barden replied, and made her eyes shoot wide when he added, 'I haven't set this up only for you to—'

Emmie stopped him right there, her feelings of being totally foxed rapidly starting to clear in that last half-sentence. 'Set this up?' It was she who challenged this time. My stars—was he a master at 'setting things up' or wasn't he?

But any scant notion which flitted into her head that Barden was again setting her up for seduction swiftly evaporated when he elucidated, 'Because it is of some—very great importance to me—I purposely rang my father and asked if he would drive over in one of his classic cars.'

'To— In order…' This was crazy. She tried again. 'So he should give Aunt Hannah…' It didn't make sense.

'So you and I could have a—talk.'

That didn't make sense either. But what did? Her heartbeat was racing like an express train. 'Talk?' she questioned, with what few wits she could find.

'We need to discuss a few matters, Emily Lawson—you and I.'

'Discuss?' She knew she was sounding like a parrot—but that was how she was starting to feel—bird-brained.

'Our discussion has waited much too long from my point of view.'

She strove to string a sentence together. 'You—you're—um—not due back for another week,' she reminded him, knowing that had got nothing to do with it, but it was the best she could manage.

'I came in a hurry,' Barden replied. And very nearly shattered her completely, when he added, 'I came in a hurry—to see you.'

She wasn't sure her mouth didn't fall open. 'You came—to see me!' she exclaimed. And suddenly all her instincts were on guard. She might not be doing very well in the intelligence department just then. But all her instincts were alert and telling her that the womanising swine was up to something. Oh, very definitely he was up to something—a pity she wasn't playing!

CHAPTER EIGHT

'WELL I'm not here to see you!' Emmie stated belligerently. Confound it! He thought he could set her up and she'd go along with it! 'I'm here to collect Aunt Hannah!' she told him firmly. He could play what game he liked—she hoped he liked solitaire. 'I don't know why you've gone to—to the lengths you have to—to…and I'm not in the slightest interested,' she inserted heatedly, lest he should think differently. 'But—but…' She was running out of steam. 'But I think it's diabolical of you to make an elderly lady get into a t-taxi and come over h—'

'Mrs Whitford didn't arrive by taxi,' Barden cut in mildly, his eyes seeming very watchful.

Emmie knew her agitation was showing—well, why wouldn't it? 'Well, it's for sure she never walked it!' she erupted.

'I do wish you'd calm down, Emmie. I'm fully aware of your fiery temper, but we'll get nowhere…'

'In case you hadn't noticed, I'm not interested in getting anywhere with…er—where you're concerned,' she blew. Oh, grief, she'd nearly said 'with you'. But what the heck was he meaning anyway?

She turned her back on him and tried to find some semblance of calm. She needed to be calm; she had nearly slipped up in temper then and coupled them together. She couldn't afford such slips. She just wanted to collect Aunt Hannah and get out of there.

'Look,' Barden addressed her back—patiently for him, she realised. 'Mrs Whitford isn't going to be back for quite a while yet. Why don't you take a seat? We could use the time while we're waiting to…' He hesitated—that wasn't like him; Emmie didn't like it. 'To iron out a few misunderstandings,' he continued.

Emmie didn't like that any better. She hadn't misunderstood a thing. For heaven's sake, they'd both been near naked! What was there to misunderstand about that? Had it not been for that phone call at that timely moment—or untimely moment, depending on your viewpoint—Barden's last little set-up would have worked a treat.

She turned to face him then, her anger renewed. Apparently she still wasn't going to be allowed to go outside and wait for Aunt Hannah. Emmie took a few paces away from him—it seemed ridiculous, suddenly, to stand glaring at him for the next sixty minutes, or however long it took for her step-relative to return. She went over to one of the sofas and, as he had earlier invited, took a seat.

She was not too happy when Barden, looking pleased at his small victory, came and pulled up a chair not two yards away. 'So, if Aunt Hannah didn't come by taxi, how *did* she get here?' Emmie demanded to know. He wanted to talk, to discuss? They'd talk all right, but only about matters *she* wanted to raise.

Knowing him, however, and his get-to-the-bottom-of-everything kind of brain, she had to own to feeling a mite surprised when he allowed her that same right. Instead of embarking on his own discussion, he answered her.

His answer, however, stunned her into a brief silence when, his eyes on her, he stated, 'I drove her here.'

She stared at him, blinked, and managed a two-word sentence. '*You* did?'

'I may have mentioned that I wanted to—discuss...' There it was, that hesitation again—as if he was selecting his words very carefully! '...something, with you,' he continued slowly, going on to stun her further when, having—skilfully, it seemed to her—brought the subject away from what she wanted to discuss, he added, 'I called at your flat early on this morning—you weren't in.'

'You called at…' Her brain seized up momentarily. She just couldn't get the hang of this. Barden could have practically any woman he chose. His desire for her in particular wouldn't have him going to these extraordinary lengths, would it? 'I—er—was out shopping,' she said witlessly, while she mentally scoffed at the notion that Barden was so desirous of a fling with her that he had raced home from the States a week early to get it under way. For goodness' sake, wake up, do!

'I know,' Barden commented—but she was at a loss to know *what* he knew. 'It was—urgent that I see you,' he stated, which didn't help. 'When you weren't in I went to call on Mrs Whitford.'

Emmie's brain started to stir. 'You went to ask her where I was?'

'I didn't get to see her then, but I saw a care assistant who remembered me from that time we dropped Mrs Whitford back at Keswick House.' Oh, don't remind me! Aunt Hannah had referred to him as her 'granddaughter's fiancé'. 'She told me that Mrs Whitford was chairing a meeting and that she didn't have the nerve to interrupt unless it was dreadfully important—and would it wait until my fiancée collected her grandmother that afternoon?'

Spare my blushes, why don't you! 'You want me to apologise again for that?' Emmie asked shortly.

'How could I when you blush so beautifully?' Barden asked softly.

She almost smiled—then realised she was being seduced! 'Cut that out, Cunningham!' she snapped, refusing to blush ever again.

'You're beautiful,' he said quietly, but before she could fire up again he continued, 'I was heartily relieved after my visit to Keswick House to know that you hadn't gone away somewhere for the weekend, but—'

'Relieved?' Emmie questioned, deciding it was time she bucked her ideas up. Barden was clever; she'd seen him in action. But just because she craved to be in his arms, that didn't mean she was all weak and feeble and ready to give in. She would fight it, and him, all the way. Challenge him all the way—because she was now growing more and more convinced that Barden was either building her up so he could drop her down again from a great height—though why he would do that she hadn't worked out yet—or he was on the way to asking her to have an affair with him. She loved him too much to be able to bear it when, as would happen in a very short space of time—she knew it— he would move on to the next refusing, and therefore challenging, female in his orbit.

'I have a meeting in New York on Monday—it's important to the company and its employees that I be there.'

'You're going back to the States?' she questioned seriously.

Barden looked at her steadily. 'I flew back only to see you, Emmie,' he said.

Her heart, which had been beating erratically since he had opened the door to her, gave a lurch, and another excited racing beat. 'W-when did you arrive?' she stammered.

'I flew in on Concorde last night,' he replied.

He'd said he had come in a hurry to see her, but—in *that* much of a hurry? She was starting to be more confused than ever! Perhaps she'd got it all wrong. Barden flying home wasn't about business, by the sound of it. But surely a man of his standing, his sophistication, wouldn't break into an important two-week business trip to jet home on Concorde merely because he wanted an affair with *her*?

'You flew in last night, you said?' she recapped, feeling her way.

'I did,' he agreed firmly, his eyes ever watchful on her.

'Forgive me for being slow—I'm feeling a mite confused here,' she confessed.

'Take all the time you need,' he invited kindly, surprisingly kind for a man in such a hurry—though he did seem a trifle pleased to see that she had, for the moment, lost her fiery edge.

'And you flew in to—only to talk to me, to have a discussion with me?' She was still feeling her way.

'I felt it vital—feel it of the utmost importance—to have—a discussion with you, Emmie.'

She was starting to melt again. He only had to say her name in that gentle-sounding way and she was about to crumble. But this would never do. 'Don't they have telephones in New York?' she asked sharply. My stars, he'd had her going there for a moment!

'They do, and if you remember I tried that. Last Wednesday I rang—and had the phone slammed down in my ear for my trouble.'

So this *was* about business. Emmie didn't know if she was disappointed or what she was, but her anger with him was on the loose again when she flared hotly, 'If you've come personally to offer me my job back out of pity again, you can jolly well—'

'Pity!' he broke in, seeming amazed that she had put that interpretation on his phone call. 'I don't pity you, you proud nitwit.'

'Thanks!'

'You're sweet and kind and uncomplaining of your lot, and I admire you tremendously.' Oh, she wished he wouldn't; she was feeling all shaky inside again. 'But never have I pitied you,' he went on, then hesitated, began again, 'I...' Then he seemed to change his mind, and said, 'I rang because I needed to talk to you. To open with a small discussion on work seemed at the time to be quite a good introduction to—'

'When have *you* ever been backward about coming to the point?' She managed to find sufficient backbone to challenge him.

'Never—until I met you. I didn't know what nerves

were—until you came along,' he half pole-axed her by saying.

Emmie stared at him in amazement. She admitted he seemed to hold the exclusive rights on scattering her brain-power, but was he truly saying that he had needed an introductory subject because he'd been *nervous* about coming to the point?

'You—um—surprise me,' was about all she could find to say. Surprised? Dumbfounded, more like!

'I've surprised myself countlessly since I've known you,' Barden revealed. And it was all too much. He was trying to tell her something here. She didn't know what it was; she had gone past hoping to be able to work it out.

'I'm—listening,' she mumbled. It was the small encouragement he had been looking for.

'After that phone call—that disastrous phone call when you more or less told me I could forget any idea of your coming back to work for me—I knew then that as much as needing to talk to you I—needed to *see* you.'

Warily she stared at him. 'You needed to—see—me?' she checked.

'I almost rang you back and asked you to fly out to me.'

Stunned, her eyes huge in her face, she looked at him. 'But—you decided against it?'

'I had to. I'd been thinking in terms of asking you to join me in your PA capacity.'

'Naturally.'

He allowed himself a half-smile. 'Naturally,' he agreed. 'But you'd just as good as told me you'd starve before you'd come back to work for me. And it was then that I knew I was done with pretence anyway.' He broke off to study her seriously for some long moments. And then, after that short while, 'I wanted to see you—because you're you, Emmie,' he stated quietly, his eyes holding hers, searching hers as if seeking some kind of reaction. Numbly, Emmie stared back. 'Which is why I flew in last night—to see and to talk to you.'

Emmie coughed to clear a suddenly nervous throat. 'And—it has nothing to do with work?' she asked, feeling her way again.

'Not one solitary thing,' Barden assured her.

And suddenly, with what sense of comprehension he had left her with, Emmie realised she had been right in her first supposition. 'I'm sorry to disappoint you, Barden—' she began, as steadily as she could, doing her best to keep things civil, polite.

'*Disappoint!*' The word seemed strangled from him; he even seemed to her eyes to have lost some of his colour. 'You're saying you aren't interested in—'

'I'm not!' she interrupted quietly, loving him so much it hurt—as did it hurt to see how his jaw tensed, as if he was striving for some kind of control. 'I can't have an affair with you…'

'*Affair!*' he exclaimed, startling her by the strength of his tone. 'Who the hell's asking you to have an affair?' he demanded.

And that was just the end for Emmie—she'd got it wrong. She had determined never to blush again—but she blushed furiously to the roots of her hair. 'I'm sorry!' she gasped, shooting to her feet and diving for the door. 'I'll go and wait in my car!'

She was at the door when Barden caught her. She struggled to be free—he refused to let her go. 'Be still.' He tried to hush her.

'Let me go.' She struggled and pushed, but found she was going nowhere.

'Not yet—not ever, you daft crackpot.'

Emmie stilled, found the nerve to pull back and look at him. He was looking encouragingly down at her. She wanted to question that 'not ever' but couldn't, so she repeated, 'Daft crackpot?'

'Forgive me.' He smiled. 'But you did get it all so wrong.'

'I…' She couldn't finish.

'Don't be embarrassed, little love,' he urged gently, and she was glad he was still holding her because that 'little love', even without his gentle tone, was threatening to turn her legs to water.

'I'm—sorry. I got it wrong,' she said, with what dignity she could muster.

'The fault is mine,' he accepted. 'This is new territory for me. Take that, and a pinch of nerves—and I'm succeeding in making a total hash of everything I've rehearsed since I made up my mind to come and g— see you.' Helplessly, her heart once more reacting like crazy, Emmie stared at him. 'Be kind to me, Emmie,' he requested. 'And give me the chance I need to tell you what it is I *do* want.'

If it wasn't work, and it wasn't an affair… Her brain seemed stymied, unable to take her any further. But, since she was no longer struggling or resisting, Barden, keeping one arm about her, as if still not convinced she would not bolt, turned her back towards the sofa.

He seated himself next to her this time, and Emmie, striving to get herself together, pulled out of his arm. Not that it did much good. He was so dear to her, and so close.

He half turned in his seat so he could look at her. 'To save any more misunderstandings, Emmie, I'll start at the beginning. But first of all I think I've got to bite the bullet, and risk you laughing your beautiful head off, by telling you that…' He took a long breath, and then, to her utter astonishment, very clearly said, '…that—I love you.'

Emmie stared at him solemnly, in shock at what he had just said, while every scrap of intelligence she possessed was battling to take it in. He loved her—oh, the joy if that was true. She had always known him honest and straightforward, but—despite his vehement denial—was it really an affair he wanted after all? Was 'I love you' just the way

he went in pursuit of a conquest? She had no way of knowing. What she *did* know, though, was that she did not want
to be just another of his conquests.

'You're not laughing,' he said.

She was afraid to give him too much encouragement in
case he saw how it was with her. And yet if he did care
for her, as he said, and this wasn't all part of the 'affair'
scenario, she just had to find out more of his 'love' for her.

She found her voice—albeit that it was so husky suddenly it didn't sound like her voice at all. 'That's probably
because I'm not experienced in these matters.'

'That makes two of us.' He smiled.

Emmie felt on extremely shaky ground. 'Er—when—
um—did it start?' she wanted to know, looking at him,
trying to gauge him, trying to use her brain and not her
heart. 'This…' She coughed; the word 'love' had got stuck.
'This—um—caring…?'

Barden took over. 'There am I, sitting at my desk one
Tuesday, with a job application form in front of me completed by a Miss Emily Lawson. On the face of it she was
eminently suited for the position. Would her voice match
up?'

'No point in having an efficient assistant PA if she's got
a voice like Donald Duck,' Emmie murmured. So far, so
good. Though she felt overwhelmingly stressed to know
more of Barden's stated 'I love you'—oh, he couldn't,
could he?—she felt she could cope in these neutral waters.
He might, of course, only be talking to get her to feel more
comfortable with him before he went for the big crunch of
telling her what all this was about. But for the moment she
was prepared to go along with him. 'So, you—um—invited
me for interview?'

'I knew you had a lovely voice. The surprise was that
you were equally lovely,' he commented. 'Even if you so
nearly didn't get the job.'

'There were other applicants just as well qualified?' Emmie supplied.

'True, but that wasn't the reason. I knew you were hiding something when I put that question about commitments.'

'Did you?' she gasped.

'You're not a very good liar.'

'I do my best,' she said, and he smiled—almost as if he loved her. But she mustn't think about that; the let-down would be too intolerable.

'I should have ruled you out there and then,' Barden continued. 'Normally I would have. But I was just about to discover that nothing I thought of as normal would ever be normal again.'

'Because—of me?'

'Oh, yes, because of you,' he replied. 'There you are at interview—pleasant, in a detached kind of way, but hiding something. I should have known then—when I went against my better judgement and took you on—that I was taking on trouble.'

'Trouble?' she questioned. 'I didn't think there was too much wrong with my work.'

'There was nothing at all the matter with your work,' he told her. 'In fact you were very soon proving you were every bit as good as you'd said you were. The trouble you caused me had nothing to do with work.'

'You're saying—er—that I was trouble to you—personally?' she questioned nervously.

'From day one,' he confirmed unhesitatingly. 'Your aloofness I could just about go along with—in fact I told myself it was preferable than to have someone in my office who was over-friendly. But your colossal arrogance was something else again.'

'You're referring to my getting it all wrong about you and Roberta Short?' Emmie guessed, and confessed, 'I thought you were going to sack me when we had that row.'

'And I couldn't think why the hell I hadn't—though of course I know why now.'

Emmie shot him a startled look. Was he saying—because he loved her? She wanted oh, so very badly to believe that. But it still seemed much too incredible to be true—she needed to hear more, much more. She needed to question, and pry—with what intelligence he'd left her.

'I think I did apologise—eventually,' she commented, and when Barden returned her look unwaveringly she felt she had to explain. 'I'd—er—had my fill of womanising employers. With all those women ringing you up, aside from the fact that into the bargain I was soon certain you were having an affair with your friend's wife, I...'

'You thought I was set in the same mould,' he inserted gently.

Remembering Karla, she still didn't know that he wasn't. 'Karla Nesbitt.' The name seemed to leave Emmie's lips before she could stop it.

'Is no longer—' He broke off. 'You're jealous?' he questioned quickly, and appeared to take tremendous heart from that notice.

'Not at all!' she denied crisply. Oh, watch it, Emmie, watch it, do. He's smarter than you by half—do you really think he could be in love with you?

She saw his expression become deeply serious. But again, to her surprise, that patience she had noticed in him earlier was there again, when, after a moment or two of just studying her, he asked softly, 'Would it be of any help if I mentioned that I've been half off my head with jealousy over you?'

Her eyes shot wide. 'No!' she gasped. 'Who?' she asked, not believing it for a minute. For pity's sake—who did she see?

'Trust me?' Barden requested. 'First there's Jack Bryant, annoying me when within hours of meeting you he's asking you for your phone number. Then...'

'But—but that was ages ago! You're not saying you were—jealous of Jack...?'

Barden smiled at her stunned expression, and owned, 'I wasn't admitting to myself then that it was more jealousy than annoyance.'

'But—you think it was?'

'I know it was. We'd had a row the day before, you and I, and from that moment it seemed you were forever coming between me and my work. Devil take you, I thought— yet found you were in no time turning my world upside down.'

Her mouth fell open a little. 'I—was?'

'You were.'

Emmie swallowed. She wanted to believe—dared she believe? She needed to know more. 'G-go on,' she invited huskily.

Barden needed no further invitation. He moved his position on the sofa to sit closer to her still, and began to tell her of the upside-down world she had made for him. 'Why, when I found I wanted only your good opinion, was I behaving in the exact opposite way? Being as aloof with you as you'd been with me? Damned if I'd explain about the surprise party Roberta Short had asked my aid with. How dare this beautiful assistant PA pass judgement on me? Hell, without you having to say a word there you were, your disapproving looks saying it all! I hadn't had my wrists slapped since childhood.'

'I made you angry.'

'I found you—irksome. But it was too late then to get rid of you. I couldn't, you wretched woman—there was something about you that was getting to me.'

'Oh.' A hint of a smile was coming through. Barden spotted it immediately, and seemed encouraged by it.

He wasted no time in going on. 'From that first day, dear Emmie, I was drawn to you. Which meant, love being the perverse animal it is, that when I wanted you to only see me in a good light I seemed only able to let you see the opposite.' He shook his head slightly, as though still a little mystified by the whole of it. 'Logic, my dear, walked out of the door the day you walked in.'

'But—you're the most logical man I've ever met!'

'What can I tell you? You, thoughts of you, kept insinuating their way into my head, and I'd find while at times I was astonished by your kindness and sweetness, at others I was furious with this prim and proper little miss.'

'I thought you were two-timing your friend, and then, when all those women rang up, two-timing your friend's wife.'

'Were you just a bit jealous?' he wanted to know. 'Just a tiny bit?'

'Angry,' Emmie admitted. 'I was angry...' She looked at him. He was rather wonderful, and he was giving so much—would it hurt to give back, just a small fraction? 'Angry and, on reflection,' she owned, 'a wee bit jealous.'

'Little love.' Barden caught hold of one of her hands and brought it to his lips and kissed it. 'I'm not a saint, Emmie, I don't profess to be, but those phone calls were, with one exception, in response to the invitations Roberta had sent out. You—um—didn't seem to notice that twice as many *men* as women phoned me with their acceptances?' he teased, and she had to laugh. She had put those male calls down as business calls.

But he'd said 'with one exception'. 'Karla Nesbitt,' she said, laughter gone.

'Karla and I went out a few times. But I had to tell her last Sunday, when she turned up at my home uninvited to wish me Happy Landings, that I wouldn't be seeing her again.'

'You've—finished with her?'

'To be frank—and I want only openness between you and me—there wasn't a lot to finish. It doesn't reflect well on me, I know, but because of the openness I want I have to tell you I only went out with Karla a few times—and then mainly because you had, by then, taken complete possession of my every waking thought.'

'I—had?'

'You had,' he agreed. 'This was all new to me, Emmie. It made me vulnerable—I didn't like it.'

'I'm sorry,' she smiled.

'I love you,' he said.

'Oh, Barden,' she whispered tremulously.

'You—love me?' he asked, his eyes on her eyes, seeming as if they would penetrate her very soul.

She couldn't tell him. Nerves were taking great enormous bites at her. She shook her head. 'I...' Words failed her.

'You don't!' he exclaimed hoarsely.

'I...' she tried again.

'You're not ready yet?' His eyes searched her face, as though trying to read her answer. 'So—what else can I tell you of the anxiety and jealousy you've stirred in me?' he asked. 'Shall I tell you how, on the very morning Personnel deliver a clutch of dreadful references from your previous employers stating your rudeness—and didn't I have first-hand knowledge of your astonishing impudence?—and referring to your erratic time-keeping you don't turn up at all?'

'You were so angry,' Emmie recalled.

'Why wouldn't I be? Dawn had phoned in and was suffering. I'd said not to come in, so there am I, minus PA *and* assistant PA. If I'd wanted proof of your erratic time-keeping—I had it. I tried to phone you, but...'

'You did?'

'You weren't answering. Either you'd left for the office or you were in bed and didn't want to get out of it. Your references were not lying. And I was not liking you at all, my dear Emmie, when you eventually turned up and gave me that "domestic problem" for an excuse.'

'It showed,' she murmured.

'I was a swine to you,' he said contritely. 'After all the anxiety you must have been through until you found Mrs Whitford too.'

'You didn't know about Aunt Hannah then.' Emmie smiled.

'Which doesn't make me feel the least bit better that—when I didn't *need* those minutes of the Stratford meeting—I, out of sheer bloody-mindedness, all but caused you to catch pneumonia by insisting you get them typed back and delivered to me at Neville Short's house that evening.'

'Pneumonia's a bit of an exaggeration,' she murmured, then asked, 'You didn't need them?'

'Sheer bloody-mindedness,' he repeated. 'How was I to know you'd trudge through the snow to get them to me? But I should have known—I'd seen and admired your spirit.' Her backbone was so much water again. 'I shall never forget seeing you standing there that night—blue with cold.' He risked a gentle kiss to her cheek. 'Your loyalty alone redeemed your dreadful references,' he said softly. Emmie, a kind of trembling going on inside her, was incapable of speech, and Barden, perhaps taking heart that she wasn't moving away after the liberty of his kiss, looked into her wide brown eyes and told her, 'I think, looking back, that it was that night that I started to fall in love with you.'

Emmie swallowed. Oh, she loved him so. She was going to burst if he said much more. 'I—w-woke you up—puking,' she stammered, needing to inject a stern dose of reality into the conversation if she wasn't to hurl herself into his arms.

'And I,' he took up, 'who'd never thought the day would come which would see me holding someone's head while they parted with their stomach contents, felt quite overwhelmed by the feeling of wanting to protect you which came over me.'

'Oh, Barden,' she whispered.

'Sweet Emmie,' he breathed, his look on her so tender she just couldn't doubt that he had some caring for her. And her heart was racing when he revealed, 'That protective feeling for you stayed with me the next day, as I drove you home—though naturally I told myself that it was only because you'd been so ill during the night.'

'Naturally,' she murmured, and at last a feeling of belief in the warmth of his love was starting to come through.

'I knew, of course, when we reached your flat that you, shocking liar that you are, were avoiding telling me something.'

'Aunt Hannah.' Emmie smiled.

'Aunt Hannah,' he agreed. 'I wish I'd known about Mrs Whitford when, feeling fidgety that you might still be unwell, I rang you that evening. You said you had company—and I was as jealous as hell.'

'You weren't!' she gasped—though she clearly remembered how the line had gone dead immediately after she had told him she had company.

'I was sure it was some man.' He smiled. 'Not that I was admitting *then* that I was jealous. Heaven forbid—that sort of thing doesn't happen to me. So why am I again suffering the same emotion when, the following Monday at the office, you get a phone call and ask for an hour off and I immediately think it's some man? Why, if it's not jealousy, do I feel all uptight when I see your old neighbour kissing you? And I'm still in the silent throes of wondering what the devil's the matter with me when you're introducing me to Mrs Whitford and I'm starting to realise what a truly wonderful person you are.'

'Oh, Barden, I'm not,' she whispered, loving him so much, wanting only his good opinion, but— She became aware suddenly that something of her feelings for him might be showing in her eyes, for, ever alert, a new sort of light seemed to enter his.

'When did you know?' he asked quickly.

'What?' she answered, totally foxed for the moment.

'That you loved me,' he answered.

'It was—' She broke off, horrified, too late—he was not about to let her off the hook, not now.

He smiled, the most fantastic loving and giving smile she had ever seen. 'You do!' he exclaimed in delight. 'Oh, my love, you do! I've so hoped. I thought last night when I lay sleepless that perhaps you might, that I might have seen—then I was sure I hadn't. But you do, don't you? You do love me, Emmie, don't you?'

He seemed to be almost pleading—how could she deny him? 'I—d-do,' she managed, from a strangled kind of throat. It was all he waited to hear.

The next second she was in his arms, being held up against him. Held and held, and adored. 'This past week's been hell,' he murmured against her hair, and then, pulling back and looking deeply into her eyes, 'Say it, dear love,' he pressed, 'and put me out of my misery.'

What could she do? 'I love you,' she replied tremulously—and was rewarded by the most loving and adoring kiss.

Barden refused to let her go, still held her in his arms, drawing back so he could feast his eyes on her. 'When?' he insisted on knowing.

Emmie smiled. Oh, never had there been such a wonderful feeling as knowing that the one you loved loved you. 'It crept up on me while I wasn't looking,' she answered shyly.

'I know all about that one.' He nodded, and, as if he still couldn't believe it, bent nearer to touch his lips to hers. 'When did you get the first inkling?' he wanted to know.

She could hold back no longer. 'I suppose something started very early on,' she answered openly. 'I certainly wasn't liking that bevy of females who rang you—though I didn't consider my dislike might be jealousy. I was certain

I didn't care for the fact it seemed I was again working for a womaniser.'

'Oh, sweetheart—I got that sort of thing out of my system in my late teens.'

'Did you?' she asked.

'Poor love, you've had a bad time of it, haven't you?' he sympathised gently. 'Believe me, darling, I left that kind of thing behind years ago, when I learned to prefer more substance in a relationship.'

'Have there been many?' She immediately wished she hadn't asked the question, but it was out now.

'Relationships?' he replied. 'A few, over the years,' he allowed, ready, it seemed, to answer her every question. 'But all over now—and none of them were like you and me, Emmie.' He kissed her gently. 'You've absolutely nothing to be jealous of.'

She believed him, knew she could trust him, and returned his smile. 'Jealousy seems to go with the territory.'

'Tell me about it!' he commented. 'But you're not telling me what I need to know, little Emmie. I've just stated I'm a grown man—but I've got this terrible anxiety to be assured that you love me.'

She had to smile again. Indeed the whole of her being seemed to be wreathed in a smile. But she knew the feeling Barden was going through, of needing to be assured of love, so she wasted no more time and told him, 'I love you, Barden Cunningham—and I hardly know why.'

'Tell me more,' he ordered.

'You've been a bossy pig a lot of the time,' she informed him lovingly.

'I'm not sure I want to hear that bit.' He smiled—as if he too felt a mass of burgeoning smiles.

'And yet, at the same time, you've been unbelievably kind.'

'I like this better,' he murmured, and Emmie looked at him. Gathering her nerve, she just had to lean forward and kiss him. 'Oh, Emmie, Emmie, I love you so,' he said against her mouth—and she thought she might burst into tears from the sheer joy of it.

She swallowed hard on a knot of emotion and pulled back. She swallowed again, and was then able to resume. 'I thought you'd dismissed me—given me the sack that Monday you discovered all about Aunt Hannah—and yet you didn't. We went back to work, and that evening you gave me a lift to collect my car, and...'

'I certainly wasn't having any David-cum-Adrian muscling in!'

'You—were jealous—of Adrian?' she asked in surprise, remembering then that she had originally arranged for Adrian to take her to collect her car.

'I wasn't calling it jealousy,' Barden answered with a self-deprecating look. 'To my mind it was the least I could do, since your car had only gone off the road when you were doing business for me. Though I wasn't entirely thrilled, I have to admit, when earlier Mrs Whitford asked were you going to marry him.'

'There was never any question of that,' Emmie promised.

'So why were you and he all lovey-dovey and shopping together this morning?' Barden startled her by asking seriously.

'We weren't!' she answered.

And she actually saw Barden blanch at what he thought he knew to be an outright lie. 'I saw you, Emmie,' he stated, oh, so dreadfully quietly.

'Me—and Adrian—shopping?'

'You were both carrying plastic bags of shopping—this morning, outside your flat,' he reminded her. And suddenly Emmie knew what he was talking about.

'We hadn't been shopping!' she exclaimed, going on quickly—anything to take the hint of doubt from Barden's face, 'Adrian has the flat above mine, and—'

'Does he?'

'Didn't you know? That's how he came to be calling that morning—after you slept in Aunt Hannah's bed. He'd probably come down to borrow something—he does sometimes. Anyhow,' she rushed on, 'he's still very much in love with his ex-live-in-girlfriend. He had just finished talking to her on the phone, having got her to agree to go out on a date with him, when he saw me coming home from his window. He couldn't wait to tell me his good news—he just had to tell someone...'

'So he dashed downstairs, grabbed a hold of some of your shopping—and gave you a kiss,' Barden finished for her. 'Jealousy,' he stated, that look of doubt gone, 'is a monster of an emotion.'

'Oh, Barden,' she sympathised softly. 'Er—just a... Didn't you say you'd called at my flat and I wasn't in?'

'You weren't—the first time.'

'You called twice?'

'Once I'd been able to ascertain that you weren't planning to be elsewhere for the weekend, I called back.'

'But you didn't stop and—?'

'What—with you and the dastardly Adrian exchanging kisses on the pavement?' He smiled.

'Oh, Barden, is that how it seemed?'

'Like I was so blindingly jealous I had to get out of there, lest I came over and threw him over the basement railings.'

'Ooh!' she exclaimed in awe.

'I got out of there, jealousy at my gut—what had been going on while I was away?'

'Nothing,' she answered.

'I know,' he said tenderly. 'Just as I know I'd no right to be jealous. I hadn't declared my love for you, or anything like that. But if what I'd witnessed was anything to go by I was *never* going to get the chance to tell you how I feel about you. Nor, I realised, as I began to calm down, was I going to have the chance to find out if the glimpses of your caring for me that—on dissecting your every nuance—I'd made myself believe I thought I'd seen were real. And I wasn't having that.'

'You weren't?'

'Sweet darling, I'd come home especially because I couldn't take not knowing any longer. I wasn't going back until I'd seen you alone and had the chance to talk to you.' He paused. 'It was then that I devised my devious plan.'

Emmie laughed; she had to. Who, loving him the way she did, could not? 'I love you,' she said, and Barden promptly delayed telling her of his devious plan by gathering her close and kissing her. For ageless loving moments they just stared lovingly at each other. 'Devious plan?' she reminded him dreamily.

Barden took time out to gently kiss her again, and then, collecting his thoughts, began to reveal, 'I was furious, jealous, sick—anything you care to name as I accelerated past your flat. But as my world started to right itself I knew I couldn't take any more—my emotions over you were crucifying me, dear love. I'd made myself believe you may have a little caring for me—but now...' Emmie gently kissed him, and he smiled, squeezed her to him, and continued. 'Nerves, by this time, were starting to set in—previously, I hadn't needed a reason to come and call on you, this time my vulnerability was raw. My first plan was to return to Keswick House and, if Mrs Whitford was willing, take her for an early lunch, and then, excuse ready-made, deliver her to your place.'

'You decided to take Aunt Hannah to lunch?'

'I had to do *something*.' He smiled. 'Though when I looked at my plan for snags one very large one was glaringly obvious. I was desperate for some private conversation with you—it would hardly be private with Mrs Whitford there.'

'So you went on to devious Plan B?'

He grinned. It was a joyous grin, and Emmie fell in love

with him all over again. 'I called at Keswick House and invited Mrs Whitford to have lunch here…'

'Here at Hazeldene?'

He kissed her. 'Correct,' he said, and, clearly liking the taste of her lips, he kissed her again before resuming, 'While Mrs Whitford was up in her room, getting her coat on, I took the opportunity to nip out to my car, ring my father and tell him how vitally important it was to me that he drove over to take an elderly lady for a tour around in one of his classic cars.'

'He—er—didn't mind?'

'He knows me—knows I wouldn't use the words "vitally important" unless I meant them,' Barden answered, going on to reveal, 'I had a few panicky moments when, after lunch, Mrs Whitford asked if we might get back because you would be calling for her soon. It's all right,' he quickly assured Emmie, 'she wasn't alarmed in any way, and quite happily accepted it when I told her that you would be picking her up from here, not Keswick House.'

'You were certain I'd come here for her?'

'Oh, sweet Emmie, you're so protective of the old dear. I was absolutely certain of it when I made sure she wrote this address in the "Out" book.'

'Rogue!'

'Desperately in love,' he corrected, and they smiled lovingly at each other as Barden ended, 'You needn't worry about her, you know. She was off like a shot the minute she first heard and then saw the Austin Healey—and my father will take excellent care of her. He was delighted with her interest in the car—they'll probably spend the whole time talking about motor engines and all things mechanical.'

They were silent, content for the moment holding each other. 'And, as deviously planned, I drove up just as you knew I would,' Emmie murmured.

'And I could hardly open the door for the importance of what I wanted to say to you—this chance I couldn't miss.'

'Has it been so very bad?'

'You've no idea,' he answered feelingly.

'Well, yes, I have, actually.' She grinned. 'It's been so emotion-tearing for you too?'

'You've had the ability to get to my emotions one way or another from the beginning.' She felt confident enough in his love to be able to confide in him.

'You told me you liked me once,' he remembered, 'Though I think we both agreed you were feeling a bit light-headed at the time.'

'That was when you came and brought me some linctus,' she recalled.

'And a few days later I find I'm totally enchanted by you when I invite myself to lunch.'

'You kissed me,' she murmured, and if she was dreaming she never wanted to wake up.

'And spent most of my time afterwards just thinking about you,' he owned.

'You took Karla Nesbitt out the other Friday,' Emmie reminded him sweetly.

He grinned. 'And spent most of that date, my jealous love, in dragging my thoughts back from *you*.'

'You say the nicest things,' she laughed.

Barden stared at her saucy mouth. 'Did I say you were enchanting? You're bewitching.' They kissed tenderly, then he was pulling back, and saying, that strain of jealousy still lurking, 'Are you still seeing the man we had to dash back from Stratford for you to see?' he asked.

'I don't remember...' she began, puzzled.

'No sooner am I coping with my annoyance that you seem quite happy to spend all day talking to Jack Bryant than you're telling me you're seeing someone later that night,' Barden reminded her.

Emmie remembered. 'Confession time: I—er—made him up,' she admitted.

'You didn't have a date?'

'I lied.' She smiled, and loved him when he smiled too, and just had to tell him, 'I knew, that night, when we were in my flat, that I was in love with you.'

Barden just sat and stared at her. 'You knew then?'

Emmie nodded. 'I'd just discovered how I felt about you—then suddenly we were kissing each other and—and...' Her voice faded.

'And I was in severe danger of losing my head when you said, "Don't", which brought me sharply to my senses.'

'You said it wasn't supposed to happen,' she recalled. 'And I knew then that already you were regretting that it had.'

'Oh, little love, I wanted to stay and make things right with you. But your lofty attitude afterwards made me realise that you'd prefer to be on your own. I was fairly shaken myself, if the truth be known.'

'Were you?'

'You were more deeply entrenched in my head than ever. But this would never do. I liked my life just as it was. Which was why I made the decision to keep everything between us only on a business footing. Only—' He broke off, that self-deprecating look there again.

'Only come Saturday you needed somewhere to rest your migrained head...'

'I'd been restless—unsettled all that day. I wasn't going to think about you any more—so I went to a party. But I wasn't in a partying mood, wasn't enjoying it, and left after a very short while. I hadn't planned to drive anywhere near to where you live. It was miles out of my way, if anything. But near to where you live was where I found myself when my head started to explode.'

'I'm glad you came to me.'

'So am I,' Barden said warmly. 'When my head started to clear, and I played everything back, I was sure you'd tenderly kissed the top of my head.'

'I—er—couldn't help it.'

'I'm glad. When I was scraping together every sign I could that you felt something for me—our mutual chemistry, a word here, a look there—I came back again and again to that kiss. I'd seen your tremendous kindness, your love and caring for Mrs Whitford—did that gentle, tender kiss mean you had a little caring for *me*?'

'You supposed it might?'

'I could only hope. After that Sunday morning you were more in my head than ever—and I, my darling, was starting to acknowledge that there was something very, very special about one Emily Lawson. Something that made it wonderful just to be near her. Then, by the middle of the next week, you didn't hesitate to put me in a black mood by daring to tell me you'd been out with some man called Simon!'

'I only went out with him the one time, and then mainly because I was jealous that you were taking Karla Nesbitt out,' Emmie confessed.

'Oh, love,' Barden murmured, and kissed her, and confessed in turn, 'I gave myself the sternest lecture that night.'

'The subject being?'

'That Emily Lawson was one beautiful woman and what did I expect—that she'd stay in nights?' Emmie began to wonder if her heart would ever stop racing. Oh, it was too wonderful just to be loved by Barden. 'That was the night I determined to get my act together. No more sulking. You had a perfect right to go out with anyone you wanted to. Only—by Friday I wanted that anyone to be me.'

'You did? That Friday before you flew to New York last Monday?'

'The same,' he agreed. 'Yet by that time I was close to being at my most vulnerable.'

Light dawned! 'You offered to take Aunt Hannah to the Motorcycle Museum!'

'Hoping you'd come with us.'

'You felt too vulnerable to ask me out direct!' Emmie gasped.

'Hell, Emmie, I've never been in love before! And anyhow, wasn't I still trying to convince myself I liked my life just as it was?'

'You're—wonderful!' She grinned, and was thoroughly kissed, so that when they broke apart she whispered, 'You were saying?' having absolutely no idea.

'I was saying how every minute apart from you was starting to become unbearable. I'm saying how bleak everything seemed last Sunday, when I would normally have been looking forward to the challenge of my two-week trip on Monday. All I could think of was you and how I wouldn't see you again for another fifteen days.'

That was exactly how *she* had been! She smiled at him, loving him. 'I smell another devious plot coming up.' Her smile became a grin.

Barden looked enchanted by her, kissed her nose, and owned, 'I could have come over to see you, of course, but how did I know the diabolical Simon wouldn't be with you—and how would I feel if he was? And might not the dastardly Adrian, with his penchant for dropping by at the most unexpected of times, drop by again? As I said—' he smiled '—I was feeling exceedingly vulnerable.'

'So instead you rang.'

'With the invention of some note-taking.'

Invention! 'You're wicked,' she berated him laughingly.

'I'll pay you back for that,' he promised, and she just had to beam at him. Life had never, ever been this good. Though as painful memory reawakened so her smile started to fade—as did some of the joy in her eyes, 'What?' Barden asked at once, his eyes full on her, not missing that something was not right. 'What are you thinking? What's wrong,

Emmie?' She didn't want to tell him—it seemed to put a blight on everything. 'Tell me!' he insisted—and she supposed it was better aired than stifled.

'That Sunday, when you phoned. Was it your intention from the start to try to seduce me?' she asked, and had her answer in his scandalised look.

That was before his vehement, 'Hell's bells, *no*! Is that what you thought—have been thinking?'

'Th-that phone call… You remember?' Oh, heavens, she was blushing again; she knew she was. 'When—'

'I know when,' he came in swiftly, to help her out. 'It was my uncle Tobin—my head was in such a mess after you'd bolted I didn't remember to ring him back until I was in the States. But what…?'

'He said…'

'What? I didn't think he said anything. I just thought you passed the phone to me and then realised where our lovemaking was leading—and panicked. But—' He broke off, and said gently then, 'Come on, Emmie, there are no secrets between us now. What did he say?'

He was right, she saw. She didn't want any secrets between them either. 'He said—and of course he thought it was you he was speaking to—he said for you to stop seducing your secretary and speak to him.'

Barden groaned. 'I'll kill him!' he threatened. 'Love him dearly though I do, I'll kill him!'

'Er—there's no need to do anything that drastic on my account.' Emmie felt then that she wanted only to make things better.

'He'll apologise. I'll tell him…'

'I'll die if you do. He doesn't know who I am, or the fact that it was me who lifted the receiver and heard what he said before I handed the phone over.'

'Oh, darling,' Barden mourned, and explained, 'I worked in Uncle Tobin's office for six weeks during my first student vacation. He's never let me live down the fact that I once made a callow play for his secretary. Oh, sweetheart, I'm sorry. I wish you'd said... Oh—what you must have thought...'

'I thought then that you'd set me up,' she admitted honestly.

'Come here,' he said gruffly, and held her close up to him while he explained, 'Little love, my sole reason for getting you to come here last Sunday was because I just *had* to see you. I hadn't the smallest intention for any of what happened to happen. My dear,' he went on, pulling back so he could see into her face, 'I'm fully aware of your inexperience—but, even while I hadn't accepted the true depth of my feelings, I thought too well of you to seduce you and then blithely fly off the next morning.' Emmie was convinced even before he followed on, 'I particularly tried to avoid igniting that chemistry that exists between us— only, as you may remember, with you so close I wasn't able to hold out for long.'

'It was mutual.' She met him halfway.

'You believe me?'

'Of course,' she answered, and they kissed tenderly.

Then he was leaning back to look into her face, and he scolded gently. 'Promise you'll never drive the way you did that night.'

'You followed me?'

'I had to deal with Karla first, though that didn't take long, and then I came after you. I backed off when—realising you knew I was following you—it looked to me as if your crazy driving would see you killing yourself in your efforts to shake me off.'

'It *was* you who rang when I got in?'

'You'd scared me half to death—I had to know you were home safe,' he confirmed. 'But my emotions were still raw; I couldn't speak to you then.'

'You left speaking to me until you were on the point of catching your plane the next day. You sounded so cool,' she remembered. 'Certainly as though you'd had a better night's sleep than I had.'

'Pretence,' he owned, and she smiled. 'There am I, wanting to speak to you nicely, and what do you do? You infuriate me by telling me you're not going to the office—that you're leaving!'

'Not for nothing,' she laughed, just so happy to be with him. 'You promptly dismissed me and we had a row.'

He smiled back. 'And I got on my plane, my mind in a furious turmoil—this woman has got me so I don't know where the devil I am. Then no sooner have we taken off than I'm realising this *isn't* where I want to be. I clearly remember thinking, You idiot—as it blindingly hit me—you idiot, you're in love with the woman!'

'Oh, how wonderful!' she sighed in delight.

'I'm glad you think so,' he growled. 'There am I, in a constant stew about you, wanting to phone you every five minutes—yet when I *do* give in to that mammoth urge you go all proud and stubborn on me, and have the utter gall to tell me you've found yourself work in someone else's office.'

'I've been working for a temping agency,' Emmie put in quickly. And was soundly kissed.

Then Barden was saying urgently, 'Emmie—Emmie, you're in my head night and day—I just can't leave without you.' And, while her heart picked up yet more speed, 'I love you, my dear heart, and want you with me,' he went on. 'Please, my love, say you'll come back with me.'

'To—New York?' she gasped, her heart fairly galloping now. 'B-but you're going tomorrow.'

'If you can't be ready in time we can catch Monday's Concorde—I can still make my eleven o'clock appointment.'

Emmie swallowed. 'I so wanted you to take me with you when I left the office on Friday. I couldn't bear not seeing you for—' She broke off, but had to quickly dampen the triumphant, joyous look that started to come to Barden's face. 'But I can't come,' she was forced to state.

'*Why?*' he wanted to know. 'Don't you love me enough?' he demanded. 'Emmie, I—'

'Aunt Hannah,' she interrupted. 'Oh, Barden, I do love you so. But I have to find a job. I can't just take time off. There's not only myself to think of. I need the security…'

'Haven't you been listening to a word I've been saying?' he demanded. 'I love you, Emmie. I adore you. My sweet darling, as my wife, you—and Aunt Hannah—will have all the security you will ever want or need.'

As his wife! She took a gasp of breath. 'Wife?' she gulped chokily.

'It goes with the territory,' Barden told her firmly. 'I've thought, eaten, slept, dreamt about you all this week, Emily Lawson,' he went on solemnly. 'I swear, now that I know you return my love, I cannot and will not take another week of it. You won't need to pack anything; you can shop for anything you need, anything you want, while I attend meetings. I know my parents will keep an eye on Mrs Whitford while we're away. We can leave their phone number for Keswick House to contact in the event she decides to break the rules. Though I've an idea my father would love to have an enthusiastic playmate he can show off his classic car collection to during the time we'll be away.' Barden shook her gently, 'But if you're in any way unhappy about any of that, then we'll take Mrs Whitford with us. Only please, please, my darling, say you'll come with me. Say you'll marry me.'

Emmie stared at him, her heart in her eyes. What could any girl say after such a speech, such a proposal? She swallowed, and looked at Barden lovingly. 'If it's not being too greedy,' she replied, 'may I say yes, to both?'

MILLS & BOON®

Next Month's Romance Titles

♡

Each month you can choose from a wide variety of romance novels from Mills & Boon®. Below are the new titles to look out for next month from the Presents...™ and Enchanted™ series.

Presents...™

THE MISTRESS BRIDE — Michelle Reid
THE BLACKMAILED BRIDEGROOM — Miranda Lee
A HUSBAND OF CONVENIENCE — Jacqueline Baird
THE BABY CLAIM — Catherine George
THE MOTHER OF HIS CHILD — Sandra Field
A MARRIAGE ON PAPER — Kathryn Ross
DANGEROUS GAME — Margaret Mayo
SWEET BRIDE OF REVENGE — Suzanne Carey

Enchanted™

SHOTGUN BRIDEGROOM — Day Leclaire
FARELLI'S WIFE — Lucy Gordon
UNDERCOVER FIANCÉE — Rebecca Winters
MARRIED FOR A MONTH — Jessica Hart
HER OWN PRINCE CHARMING — Eva Rutland
BACHELOR COWBOY — Patricia Knoll
BIG BAD DAD — Christie Ridgway
WEDDING DAY BABY — Moyra Tarling

On sale from 2nd July 1999

H1 9906

Available at most branches of WH Smith, Tesco, Asda, Martins, Borders, Easons, Volume One/James Thin and most good paperback bookshops

MILLS & BOON®

Medical Romance™

COMING NEXT MONTH

MORE THAN A MISTRESS by Alison Roberts

Anna's first House Officer job was in surgeon Michael Smith's hospital. She couldn't believe this was the same man she'd met on holiday, and parted from so badly. And Michael was no happier to see her!

A SURGEON FOR SUSAN by Helen Shelton

Susan was appalled when her sister set her up with a blind date! But Adam had been equally set up, by *his* sister. He was *so* gorgeous, why would anyone think he needed help finding a woman?

HOME AT LAST by Jennifer Taylor
A Country Practice—the third of four books.

After a year away Holly Ross felt able to come home. Many changes awaited her, not least a new stepmother. But the biggest change of all was her growing feelings for Dr Sam O'Neill, the partnership locum.

HEART-THROB by Meredith Webber
Bachelor Doctors

Peter's photo was plastered on *Hospital Heart-throb of the month* posters, embarrassing him when Anna came to work with him in A&E. She was intriguing and mysterious, and Peter couldn't help being fascinated. But he'd managed to stay a bachelor this far...

Available from 2nd July 1999

Available at most branches of WH Smith, Tesco, Asda, Martins, Borders, Easons, Volume One/James Thin and most good paperback bookshops

FREE

4 BOOKS
AND A SURPRISE GIFT!

We would like to take this opportunity to thank you for reading this Mills & Boon® book by offering you the chance to take FOUR more specially selected titles from the Enchanted™ series absolutely FREE! We're also making this offer to introduce you to the benefits of the Reader Service™ —

★ FREE home delivery   ★ FREE gifts and competitions
★ FREE monthly Newsletter   ★ Exclusive Reader Service discounts
★ Books available before they're in the shops

Accepting these FREE books and gift places you under no obligation to buy; you may cancel at any time, even after receiving your free shipment. Simply complete your details below and return the entire page to the address below. *You don't even need a stamp!*

YES! Please send me 4 free Enchanted books and a surprise gift. I understand that unless you hear from me, I will receive 6 superb new titles every month for just £2.40 each, postage and packing free. I am under no obligation to purchase any books and may cancel my subscription at any time. The free books and gift will be mine to keep in any case.

N9EC

Ms/Mrs/Miss/Mr ....Initials ....
BLOCK CAPITALS PLEASE
Surname...
Address...

....

....Postcode ....

Send this whole page to:
THE READER SERVICE, FREEPOST CN81, CROYDON, CR9 3WZ
(Eire readers please send coupon to: P.O. Box 4546, DUBLIN 24.)

Offer valid in UK and Eire only and not available to current Reader Service subscribers to this series. We reserve the right to refuse an application and applicants must be aged 18 years or over. Only one application per household. Terms and prices subject to change without notice. Offer expires 31st December 1999. As a result of this application, you may receive further offers from Harlequin Mills & Boon and other carefully selected companies. If you would prefer not to share in this opportunity please write to The Data Manager at the address above.

Mills & Boon is a registered trademark owned by Harlequin Mills & Boon Limited.
Enchanted is being used as a trademark.

THE Regency COLLECTION

Where rogues find romance

Look out for the third volume in this limited
collection of Regency Romances from
Mills & Boon® in July.

Featuring:

Dear Lady Disdain
by Paula Marshall

and

An Angel's Touch
by Elizabeth Bailey

Still only £4.99

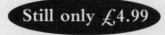

MILLS & BOON®

Makes any time special™

Available at most branches of WH Smith, Tesco, Martins,
Borders, Easons, Volume One/James Thin
and most good paperback bookshops